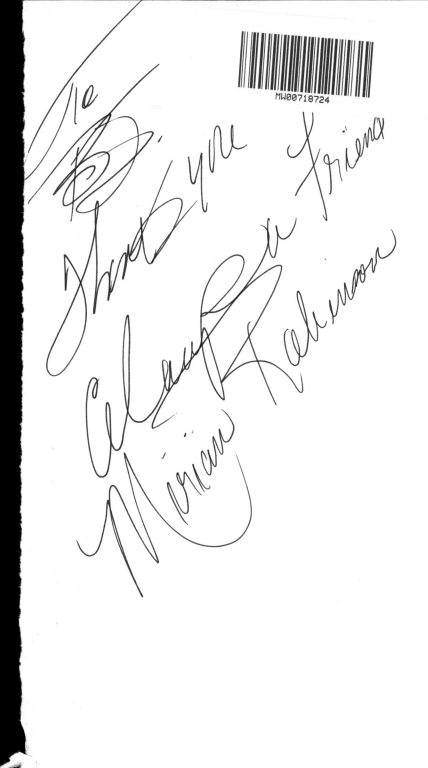

To
B.

Thank you for your friendship

Alvenia Fulmore

Marian Robinson

◆

MYSTERY OF THE BLANKET
A FICTIONAL TALE OF LIFE (...OF TRUTH)

By

Mirian Robinson

Robinson Publications

Mesquite, TX

Publisher's Acknowledgements

Designed by: Mirian Robinson
Written by: Mirian Robinson
Typed and edited by: Erbia Buggs
Cover and Design by: Donna Scott
Graphics and layout by: Donna Scott

Send all inquiries to:
Robinson Publishing
P. O. Box 1737
Mesquite, TX 75185

ISBN 0-9668684-0-4

9 780966 868401

Printed by Island Printing, Duncanville, Texas

Table of Contents

Robinson Publications

To order additional copies of
"A Fictional Tale of Life(...of Truth)
"Mystery of the Blanket,"
please contact Mirian Robinson
(972) 686-7484 or
1-800-484-5637. Code 3069

Robinson Publications
P. O. Box 1737
Mesquite, TX 75185

♦ ♦

If you can not find this book in your local stores,
you can order directly from me. Simply mail to the
address above. Include ...money order or check for
the full amount plus tax, shipping and handling.

ACKNOWLEDGEMENT

Giving praise to God Almighty for all of his wonderful blessings, and knowing that he is the answer to all of our problems...

I am grateful to each of you who over the past years encouraged me to write the second part to "Mystery of the Blanket."

Many thanks go to my husband, Clifford Robinson for his over-flowing inspiration and encouragement, as well as his dedication to support me.

To my children, I give my eternal blessings.

My warmest thanks to my editor, Erbia Buggs and my financial supporters, Kathy Walker and Donna Scott...for their belief in me.

To my mother, Mary Etta Griffin for her words of wisdom; and of course, love and many blessed kisses to my sisters and brothers.

I hope Oprah Winfrey will add my book to her Book Club list, or invite me to appear on her show.

This book is a fictional illusion of the author's imagination. The characters, incidents, and dialogues are not to be construed as real. Any resemblance to actual events or persons, living or dead, is entirely coincidental.

A fictional tale of life.....(of truth)

PREFACE

A FICTIONAL TALE OF LIFE
(...OF TRUTH)

MYSTERY OF THE BLANKET

The story follows Maggie's early years when she attended school and lived with her grandmother on the farm after her grandfather's death. Several strange episodes illustrate Maggie's growing maturity and the trouble a pretty young girl can get into. However, grandfather's blanket is always there to protect her.

The book continues on through her rocky marriage to Dan Forrest, a once loving husband who turns out to be the scoundrel everyone believed him to be, all except Maggie.

When Maggie's grandmother dies leaving the farm to her, life seems fine and good for the time being until Dan gets bored with the farm life. He tries to sell the farm without Maggie's permission. When she discovers his plans and confronts him with it, Dan goes berserk. The reader will have to take it from here. To tell too much would be to reveal the startling conclusion to a fascinating book. A true page turner, your mind will crave for more of "Mystery of the

Blanket." The short story will capture your attention and keep you on the edge of your seat throughout the final episodes. This is a profounding mystery story.

The Mystery of the Blanket contains excitement, heartfelt emotion with a touch of raw realities of life. This is combined with a dose of curiosity and suspense. You know, this mysterious tale might just have you taking a second look at all those old blankets lying around your house!!

Mirian Robinson was born and reared in Cleveland, MS in the early 1950's. Living on the farm was a simple way of life to those who loved to work the land. As the fourth child of twelve children, Mrs. Robinson was never lonely for companionship. Still, she was able to spend lots of quality time with her mother who loved to read and write short stories also. Mrs. Robinson credits her mother'' strength for keeping the large family together in times of crisis. After graduating from East Side High School, Mrs. Robinson worked at Baxter's Lab for eleven years before starting her career in cosmetology. She worked during the day and attended Beauty College at night and she eventually graduated with honors. With an undeniable spirit and true zest for life, Mrs. Robinson's creed has always been..."if you think you can, you can." If you think you can't, you are right. To rise above the seemingly obstacles that face all women today, especially black women, this creed is necessary.

The author is a member of the Southern Hills Church of Christ in Dallas, TX. She resides in Mesquite, TX with her family. This is the second novel published by Mrs. Robinson.

INTRODUCTION

I lived in a small dusty little town, about 200 miles from the state capital. We had only one Post Office. Oh yes, one grocery store and a dry good store. I remember going to the post office with my grandfather. He would walk up to the small window and knock very hard on the glass. A short little lady with light brown hair would answer after about six loud knocks. She would ask, "what can I do for you?" My grandfather would say, "I want to buy four stamps." She responded, "speak up boy," I can't hear you. I watched the expression on my grandfather's face. He hated for her to call him boy. No matter how old a person was, their name was boy or Girl. Sometimes they would call my grandmother "Auntie."

The Dry Good store sit in the middle of the town. Everybody within 30 miles came to buy items from this one store. The store sold everything you could dream about buying. I took pride in going with my grandmother at least twice a month. She had a way with herself that made me very proud hearted. Before we went into the store, my grandmother would lecture me. "Keep your hands behind you and don't touch anything, Maggie. No one can blame you if something is broken." All I could do was look. Oh, my eyes would roam over the candy and cookies displayed in the big jars on top of the counter. Sometimes Grandma would buy me a cold strawberry drink, which was my favorite soda. I would drink so slow enjoying every drop of the flavor. The store would opened up around 10 o'clock in the morning and closed at 8 in the evening. The middle of the day everyone would rush in for something cold to drink. My most favorite significant place to go was the Short Stop Café. They sold the best hamburger. Even Grandma's hamburgers were not as good as those.

The town was small, but lots of people lived there. The whites lived across the track, and the blacks lived on the other side of the track or deep in the backwoods. There were two schools in the town. Well, I guess you wouldn't say two schools, because the school I attended was in an old church building which was no longer used for worshipping. The white paint had completely peeled off. The steps had fallen down, so we used old bricks for steps. I never understood why we had to go to a raggedy old church building. The white kids went to a redbrick school with the American flag flying high over the front entrance.

The town had its way with telling you where you belonged or couldn't go. The owner of the Short Stop café was a baldheaded very fat man. He weighed over 300 pounds. I was frightened by his loud voice. Whenever a black customer wanted service, we ordered our food from the backdoor. We always had to order to go, because the owner didn't want any trouble. We had to grab our bag and get the hell away from the building. We couldn't stand around to eat or chat with our friends. Even though we were treated different, we still purchased his greasy burgers for the backdoor. One day, merely out of curiosity, I peeped into the front door. Two white girls about my age noticed me and screamed for the manager. The redheaded girl screamed, "look, look.... that nigger is trying to come inside." I ran away very fast and dropped my hamburger on the ground. I looked back and the fat man was shouting..."you stay away from this front door, you hear me girl." I never could understand why they treated us that way. Our mother took care of their children, cleaned their house and cooked for them. I wanted to despise all of them. My grandparents taught me not to hate my enemy, but to love them inspite of their rejection of us. I had to pray hard sometimes not to hate. Grandfather would say a prayer whenever he was confronted with racism. He would say, "girl, its time to stand still and fight off the devil."

Basville community was majority white. They gave us hell 365 days a year. No matter how we bent down for them, we were never low enough. They killed us like animals, and locked us up in jail without a trial. If someone said, "yes, that's the nigger I saw walking down the road...he was coming from that direction." Well, if a store was broken into or someone misplaced something, boy, you didn't stand a chance. I especially express sadness for our young black boys between the ages of 12 and 16. They were taken from their beds in the middle of the night sometimes. Oh yes, they all packed guns even if they were not the law. If they wanted to kill somebody, one of us was killed. No trial, you were found guilty by their statement.

I remember one hot day in July, someone said that a black man raped a white girl. The whole town was in rage. The police interrogated every black family. Finally, they dragged a young black man from his bed in the middle of the night. The girl stated that her attacker was a tall black man.

The boy they apprehended was a tall very dark skinned person. He was taken to the police station and they beat him to death. The Chief of Police informed the family that he tried to resist arrest. When the family arrived to remove their son's body, his hands and feet were tied together. They gagged his mouth with a dirty rag. His face was all bloody and swollen.

Later, the white girl declared that her boyfriend had beaten her because when had gone to the movie with another boy. Nothing was done about this. The family couldn't afford an attorney. Therefore, the only thing they could do was to mourn the lost of their son and his innocence. The town would bury the news as if nothing ever happen and continue on with their lives.

One day my grandfather and I stopped to buy a hamburger. There were so many people standing around the place, we waited beside the edge of the road. The police and the ambulance arrived. Finally, we heard someone say that the café owner had killed his wife. He had cutup her body and tried to burn the body out back in the garbage dump. The neighbors had noticed him carrying several bags early that morning. They thought it was strange for him to carry out trash because he only walked when he had to. The police searched the trashcan and found pieces of his wife's body partially burned. After that, I never wanted to go to that place again. As a matter of fact, I learned to enjoy Granny's hamburgers.

There was a lot on the farm to keep a kid busy. The families would get together for a farm cookout every other month. This helps to keep the children minds from drifting away from home, or maybe getting into trouble. I was very young, but I can never forget. Even the small white children were taught at an early age that they were superior over the black children. I would always feel depressed. I never wanted to be around them. For one reason, we wee never given credit for anything positive.

I remember once my grandmother baked several pies for church. The lady she worked for wanted a pie, so my grandmother, being the good spirit person she was, gave her a couple of the pies. Instead of the lady taking the pies home to eat, she entered them in a contest winning $500. Something good came out of that deceitful move. My grandmother began baking pies to sell to her and she would pay her extra for the pies. When she came by to pick up the pies, she would she would say, "Auntie, I don't know what I would do without you." Her words always stuck in my mind in a sour way....like you wouldn't be able to do a damn thing, I thought to myself. You don't have a mind for business. You can't cook or clean your house. What would you do without my grandmother's help? Not a dam thing.

Let me tell you about the baby care. My grandmother would baby-sit for her children. When she had her first baby, my grandmother taught her how to take care of the baby's needs. She didn't even know how to hold a newborn, yet.

Her standards were very high. We were not allowed to drink from her good glassware, as she called them. When we wanted a glass of water, we had a special jar to drink from. Yes, a dam fruit jar, or maybe a milk bottle. Sometimes I would go into the kitchen when she wasn't there and eat whatever I wanted from her refrigerator. I would pour a glass of milk, using her real china, as she called them. I wouldn't let my grandmother see me doing such a thing...she would give me the beating of my life. It made me feel really good because I proved to myself that nothing would happen to her family if I drank from one of her glasses.

The things we had to endure made us stronger and we prayed everyday for hope. I truly believed in God. I remember one sunny morning my grandfather and I was picking pecans on the side of the road not bothering anyone. A truck pulled up beside us and three white guys addressed, "what are you doing out there?" one of them yelled. My grandfather politely responded, "we are picking up pecans." Another guy yelled, "I bet you're trying to steal them." Grandpa reacted, "no, these trees don't belong to no one, but God." The oldest guy uttered, "oh, sure they belong to someone, they are our trees." Grandpa would pull me closer to his side. I was scared. We prayed read hard. Suddenly it began to thunder and lighting flashed over the sky. The rain poured down as if the sky had burst open right above us. The truck sped away and scattered wet gravel in our face. My grandfather looked up to the heavenly skies and said, "Lord that was right on time." We were soaking wet. As we danced around in the rain together, we thanked God for protecting us from harm. When we returned home I told Grandma what had happened, she replied, "I felt it in my heart that you all were in trouble...so I sent up a special prayer for you."

The next day we sold our pecans in town. Of course, we didn't make a large profit off the sale of the pecans. They would always swindle us. They never paid us what the pecans were really worth. But, we never stopped. I guess that's one thing about black people, we don't give up easy. Nothing makes us sit on a stump and die. We are heavy-duty people with a strong will to survive. From that day, I grew up learning to respect and forgive others for their hostile ways.

I won't say the whole town was against black people because there were some white families that spoke up about the way things were. It made a lot of difference. Our old school was torn down. A new one was built for us. A new fast food café opened up. We were allowed to go through the front door and given permission to sit down inside and eat our food without fear. New jobs opened up for us, too. A lot of changes took place...even the schools became segregated. I can remember the first day of school. There was more fighting and name-calling. For every nigger they called us, we had a name in returned for them such as honkies and rednecks. Among a few more dirty names, it didn't take long for things to settle down because we held our ground as a strong nation.

My grandparents raised me to believe in myself and to look for the good in everyone. I grew up on the farm with my grandparents. They stored a foundation of love in my heart. The farm life made me wonder about other places. Sometimes I would sit and watch the sunset from my grandparents' front porch. The sun reflected on the water in the pond. I often though to myself, what make the colors so bright and beautiful? I spent a lot of time browsing in the woods and fishing in the big pond behind the barn. My grandfather and

I would always go walking together. He would show me his favorite hunting spots. Grandpa would bring along his dusty old blanket and cover a spot. We would sit and talk for hours. Each time we packed up to leave, he would fold the blanket very carefully. I felt as if it was time to throw the blanket away. But, I would never say that to my grandfather.

I resided with my grandmother, a wonderful person. She always cooked and sewed for the church and other people. My grandmother was a spiritual person. She believed in during what was right. She lived by the rules in the Bible, trusted in God and dealt with others as she wanted to be treated.

Her husband Jake died when he was out hunting in the woods. No one knows how the accident happened. I believe my grandfather was murdered. Back in the days, if you were black or of color, when something happened to you, they always called it an accident. My grandfather was a tall man, weighting 250 pounds. He never cut his hair, but wore it in a very long ponytail. He was a descendant from a Cherokee Indian tribe. My grandfather didn't talk very much, but kept to himself. Most of the time he was in the woods hunting or working on the farm. He didn't trust white people...especially the police. They mistook his quietness for weakness, yet they feared him and called him a crazy old half-breed. My grandfather would say, "there are only two things you have to do in life, you have to die and you have to live until you die. You make up all the rest."

I loved my grandfather very much. He was a brave man, never afraid of anything on earth, but feared God

Almighty. The people that lived there, especially the white people always said that my grandfather didn't respect the laws. They were always writing him a warning about hunting out of season or killing too many deer. We lived on my grandfather's farmland that was handed down from one generation to another.

◆

CHAPTER 1
"GRANDFATHER'S DEATH"

They never found my grandfather's gun or his blanket. When they came to tell my grandmother the news, I was in the garden picking peas. I heard my grandmother scream, "no, no, you killed him." I ran to her crying, hoping I could calm her down because of her bad heart condition. The policeman stared at my grandmother and in a snubbed tone, he uttered, "I knew one day that old man would slip and fall." Grandma asked, "how could he shoot himself in the back of the head?" The policeman spit out a mouthful of tobacco, leaving tabacco juice running down his chin. "Lady, he had an accident and that's the way we found it to be." I clinched my fists together and my lips tighten with anger. I wanted so badly to run into him with all my strength and crush his eyes out. But, instead I hugged my grandmother and helped her back into the house. She was very upset. I rushed into the kitchen for a glass of water; it was time for her medicine. I placed the water in her hand. She touched my face and said, "Maggie, they killed Jake. I know they did...it wasn't an accident. Jake was too careful with guns and he always kept the safety lock on all the time.

I was only fourteen years old at the time my grandfather was killed. The news spread around the town about his death. I was very sad, wondering what would we do now that he was dead.

The day was almost over and we decided to rest until morning. Grandma had to make arrangements to bury my grandfather. There was nothing we could do for him anymore. His life on the farm was over. He always said, "bury me on my land where I can view the house and watch over you and you grandmother." I noticed Grandma standing near the table. She picked up a pair of his gloves, holding them close to her chest. She murmured, "Jake, oh my brave Jake. I am going to miss you." She appeared very tired. I pleaded with her to get some rest. I couldn't sleep that night. I just lay in bed with my eyes open. I knew the farm wouldn't be the same without my grandfather.

The next day we walked to the Carter's farm, which was about two miles down in the village. My grandmother knocked on the door. Mrs. Carter opened the door with a sad expression on her face. She uttered, "Rosemary I heard the bad news, and I am so sorry." She invited us in and gave us a glass of water. Everyone was eating breakfast. She fixed a plate of biscuits and syrup for us. I tried to eat Mrs. Carter's biscuit. They always tasted like she mixed the flour with sour milk. I sat at the table with my grandmother. Her face was puffed from crying all night, and she looked lost and alone. I thought, why did this have to happen to my grandfather? I prayed to myself, "God please help my grandmother. Don't let her get sick from this long walk."

Mrs. Carter asked, "what can I do to help you, Rosemary?" Grandma responded, "I need you to help me bury Jake tomorrow. Maybe your boys will dig the grave for me." Mrs. Carter uttered, "now you know I won't let you down. The boys will help you."

We buried my grandfather the following Sunday, and that was the saddest day of my life. It rained all day. As they lowered my grandfather's casket into the ground, I cried hysterically. I knew I would never see him again.

After the funeral everyone went home. We stood there for awhile looking at the grave. I placed flowers on top of the freshly dug soil. We realized there were nothing more to do. I prepared vegetable soup for supper. Finally, my grandmother went to sleep after taking her medicine. I sat in the quiet room listening to the raindrops on the tin roof. Suddenly, I felt a warm feeling as if I was not alone. Maybe, the feeling you get when you think someone is watching you. I glanced around slowly thinking to myself. Maggie everything will be okay. I fell asleep on the couch.

The next morning a blanket was folded over me. Someone had taken off my shoes during the night. The blanket appeared to be my grandfather's blanket. My first thought was "my grandmother had awaken in the middle of the night to cover me up. I checked-in on her and she was still sleeping. She seemed so peaceful. I didn't want to wake her up so early. I washed my hands and face and cooked breakfast. I thought about the blanket. Suddenly, I began to understand that it had to be my grandmother. Maybe, she found the old blanket outside and forgot to tell me. I prepared a pot of coffee. I went back into the living room.

The blanket looked like the old blanket that my grandfather had used many times. I was so excited. I picked up the blanket and held it close to my chest. I wanted to scream with joy. Instead, I folded up the blanket and laid it on the couch. I wanted to run and tell Grandma. I knew she had a weak heart. I didn't want to frighten her. I decided to wait until she woke up. I peeped out the window at my grandfather's grave. The flowers had fallen over from all the rain. However, the grave looked peaceful with the little white fence around it. My grandmother wanted him buried there so she could look out the window at his grave.

The smell of coffee woke my grandmother up. She entered the kitchen walking slowly. She embraced me and said, "you are a wonderful child and I don't think I could have made it without you." I smiled and said, "sit down and eat Grandma." As she walked towards the table, she replied, "I slept so hard once my head touched the pillow. I didn't move until I smelt the coffee aroma." I thought that maybe she just forgot. Grandma looked up from her coffee, "oh Maggie, what is wrong? Why are you looking at me so strange?" I uttered, "Grandma, you got up during the night and pulled off my shoes and covered me with grandpa's old blanket." Grandma looked shocked, "what blanket are you talking about, Girl?" I answered, "grandfather's old blanket." I thought. Maybe she had found the blanket and forgot to tell me about it. Grandma declared, "that old blanket hasn't been seen since Jake died." I am sure you just dreamt the whole thing. Girl, show me the blanket. I would know that old blanket anywhere." Grandma followed me into the living room. "Where is the blanket?" The blanket was not there. Grandma asked, "are you sure you folded up a blanket, or were you just thinking about your grandfather?" I answered, "no, I was sure it was here." I remembered folding up the blanket. I thought, how could I make Grandma believe me? I was very confused. I didn't know what to think.

I finished my breakfast and began washing the dishes. Yet my mind wondered about the blanket. Grandma blabbered, "well, I don't understand how it could be there one minute and the next minute it's gone." Neither did I.

I forgot about the blanket and went to school. I had to walk a long way to school. My mind was set on getting there fast. As I walked to school, the bus passed by me. All the white kids looked out the window. They always had time to roll down the window and throw paper at me or call me nigger. I wondered sometimes why I couldn't ride the school bus with them. The bus passed right by my house. As I walked faster, the thought of the school bus quickly passed my mind. I began to think about my grandfather. He always wanted me to get a good education and be the best I could be. No matter how difficult the task might seem.

The school finally appeared upon the hilltop. I was very tired from the long walk. When I stepped into the classroom, my teacher offered me a glass of water. I smiled and took my seat with the other students.

After school, I walked home singing a melody on my way to make the time go faster. When I arrived back on the farm, I could see my grandmother looking out the window for me. I entered the back door. The smell of greens and turnips cooking filled the house. My grandmother greeted me with a hug. She uttered, "dinner will be ready soon."

Later I washed the dishes and stored the leftovers in the refrigerator. I finished all my homework and walked outside to my grandfather's grave. I cleared all the dead flowers off his grave. I promised Grandpa that I would bring some fresh flowers. I sensed my grandfather's presence all the time. Sometimes it seemed like he was not dead, but, out in the woods hunting. Grandma called for me to come inside. I whispered good-bye to Grandpa.

The next day I woke up very early. I decided to look for work to help my grandmother. She went to the market that morning. She hoped to sell some of the eggs from the farm. I peeped out the window at the big house on the hill. The house belonged to the Lewis. They were very wealthy people, and of course they were white. We hardly ever saw them in public. Half of the town belonged to them. Mr. Lewis was a tall man with long red hair. He always carried a gun in the truck with him. Mrs. Lewis was a tiny little woman with dark brown hair. She always wore her hair in a ponytail, which made her appear younger. Their two children hardly ever left the farm. I remember once, Mr. Lewis said, "you are a pretty black girl. You should be working in my house. My wife could use your help with the housework." I thought for a second, maybe I am pretty. I admired myself in the mirror. I can help Mrs. Lewis clean house. The idea sounded great to me. I combed my hair and slipped on my best dress.

I began walking towards the Lewis' farm. When I stepped into their yard, the children stopped playing games and stared at me as if I had dropped down from the sky. I observed the little girl in a wheelchair. I tried not to show how afraid I was, but my hands were shaking. I asked the little boy if Mrs. Lewis was home. With a smothered giggle he asked, "why do you want to see our Mama?" My tongue laid dry in my mouth...because I'm looking for a job," I uttered. The little girl in the wheelchair pointed her finger, "there's a black girl, there's a black girl." They both stared with curiosity in their eyes. They whispered together and suddenly the little boy ran up beside me. He pulled my dress; "will that color wash off your face?" I looked down at him. He was no more than four years old. My mouth opened, "no it won't wash off."

Finally Mrs. Lewis appeared at the door. "Okay children go back to playing." Her eyes fell upon my face. "Girl, who are you looking for? Are you lost?" I was very nervous and my voice trembled as I uttered, "my name is Maggie Johnson and I am looking for work." Mrs. Lewis wiped her hands on her apron as she eyeballed me over. "Come on inside. You are mighty young to be out looking for work. What type of work can you do?" I quickly answered, "I can iron, wash, and clean house." Mrs. Lewis gazed around the house before she answered. "Yes, I can use some help in cleaning up this big house." She moved the kids' toys from the couch. "Here, sit down. I can use some help with Bertha, too." She picked up the dolls from the floor. "Let me talk with my husband. You wait here." After a few minutes Mrs. Lewis returned. She beamed, "when can you start?" With an excited pitch in my voice, I boasted, "I can start right now."

Mrs. Lewis showed me the large kitchen and the bedrooms. The house was larger than I had expected. I couldn't believe how many bedrooms the house had. I cleaned downstairs and upstairs. The rooms looked like a tornado had struck the house. I wondered if Mrs. Lewis realized how dirty her house was. I have never seen anything so dirty. All the bathrooms looked like no one ever cleaned them.

After a couple of hours of working, I was tired. Sweat poured down my face. Mrs. Lewis never asked me to relax. She continued to add more work to the list. When I finished cleaning the house, she asked me to iron Mr. Lewis' shirt. I peeped outside and the sun was going down. I informed Mrs. Lewis that I had to go home before dark. She inspected the house with a smile on her face and said, "Maggie, you have done a beautiful job cleaning up this place." She passed me some money from the cookie jar.

I started out running towards home, but I was so tired. I wanted to get home before my grandmother returned from the market. I paused for a few minutes to catch my breath. I counted the money and to my surprise, she had given me three dollars. I worked hard enough for fifty times that amount. I was thankful to have earned that.

I arrived home before Grandma. I rushed to start dinner. In the meantime, I heard the dogs barking and knew Grandma was coming home. I opened the door for her because she appeared to be tired. I gave her a big hug. "Let me help you put up the egg crates." She uttered, "ugh, I am so beat." I asked, "are you ready to eat?" She answered, "yes, I am starving." She washed her hands and sat down at the table. Her eyes were fixed on me. She asked, "what have you been doing all day? My day at the market didn't go very well. I only sold a few eggs. No one bought anything today." I responded, "yeah, slow day." Maybe this was a good time to reveal that I had been working. "That's okay Grandma. I earned some money today." She lurked with a surprised reaction. "Working, " I blabbered out. "I have a job working for the Lewis family." She was very happy for me and placed a big kiss on my cheek. She peeped over her eyeglasses, "why girl, you are going to be just like your mother."

Grandma never talked very much about my mother. Once my grandfather said that my mother died when I was just a baby. He stated that my mother was raped by a gang of white men as she walked home from work. They shot her in the back when she tried to run away and her body was found in the woods. There were rumors around town about who killed her. Four white men were in the area hunting around the time my mother was killed. My grandfather would always pray that her killers would never find peace until the truth was spoken concerning my mother's death. Six months from the date my mother was murdered, a group of white men were out on a hunting trip when their truck skidded into a tree. All of them were killed. But, before one of them died, he confessed to the police that he was a part of the team that murdered my mother.

I was a baby when my mother died. I don't have any memories of her. I promised my grandmother that I would always be there for her, to take my mother's place in her life. Now that I have a job, I can help her with the bills.

Everyday after school, I would go to the Lewis' farm. Junior and Bertha became my best friends, especially Bertha. She was thrown from the car in an accident, which left her paralyzed. I began spending more time with her after work. She loved for me to brush her long brown hair. She wore very thick glasses. The fall affected her sight. Bertha would watch for me everyday. When she saw the top of my head, I could hear her shouting, "here comes Maggie, Mama."

After working at the Lewis' house for six months, I saved enough money to help my grandmother buy some of the things she needed. She didn't have to walk to the market anymore to sell eggs. Mrs. Lewis was very kind to me. She would always give me a few dollars extra, or some of her old dresses. Once she gave me a bottle of her perfume. She would always warn me not to speak to Mr. Lewis about the things she had given me. School was almost over. I hope Grandma would feel well enough to attend our school play.

CHAPTER 2

"A LEARNING EXPERIENCE"

After the death of my grandfather, things became difficult for my grandmother and me. We worked hard to take care of all the chores on the farm. I disliked feeding the cows the most. We couldn't afford to hire anyone to help us. Grandma's medical bills were very high. Every month, she had to have her medicine, no matter what. Her heart condition would become worse without the treatment.

Grandma was very content with cooking and cleaning. She taught me how to cook and showed me the best way to iron a man's shirt. The training really helped me. I was able to iron Mr. Lewis' shirts without any problem. They looked as if they had been sent to a professional cleaner.

I never asked Grandma about the blanket again although; I often wondered what happened. Grandpa had said many times that the blanket was special. I am a firm believer and I know that his spirit will forever watch over us.

The weather soon turned cold. Winter arrived on time. Snow covered the window and doorways. I was not able to go to work for several days. I helped Grandma put up vegetables and nuts. One day as we worked in the kitchen, we noticed a truck driving up to the farm. The truck stopped in the driveway. Mr. Lewis stepped out. He asked my grandmother if I could help Mrs. Lewis around the house because his wife was sick. My grandmother hesitated for a second and replied, "yes, she can go. Have her back before dark." I put on my boots and coat. The ride to the farm was very bumpy. I sat close to the door watching Mr. Lewis from the corner of my eyes as we entered the driveway.

Everything I remembered about the big house and the gifts from Mrs. Lewis made me happy to come back to work. Mr. Lewis opened the wooden door and I walked in slowly. I pulled off my rubber boots and hung my coat in the closet. The house was quiet. No one was downstairs. I picked up the newspaper off the floor and placed the pillows back on the sofa. Mr. Lewis went into the den and closed the door behind him. I cleaned the kitchen table and loaded the dishwasher. After I cleaned downstairs, Mr. Lewis peeped around the door and said, "ugh, Maggie, when you finish cleaning downstairs, Mrs. Lewis wants you to clean upstairs too.

As I walked upstairs, there was no sound of children playing in their room. I felt very uncomfortable because I realized Mr. Lewis had lied to my grandmother. I began to feel afraid...knowing I was alone in the house with him. I glanced around the bedroom thinking, where are the children? Mrs. Lewis, was she really sick? I checked the closet and the drawers and they were empty. At that moment I knew, Maggie Johnson you are in serious trouble.

I heard Mr. Lewis coming upstairs and I froze in my tracks. The sound of his footsteps echoed in my mind. My heart began to beat rapidly. "What am I going to do?" I ran to the window, but no one was in sight. I remembered how he eyed me the time he said I was a pretty black girl. Tears webbed in my eyes. At that very second, the doorknob turned and Mr. Lewis entered the room. The smell of alcohol stirred my sense of smell. I fumbled with the covers on the bed and pretended I didn't see him. He stood in the doorway waiting for me to look up. Finally, he closed the door behind him. I stared at him with a surprised expression on my face. "Is there something else you want me to do, Mr. Lewis, I asked?" He grinned, "well...yeah as a matter of fact, there is something I want you to do."

He pulled off his shirt and his pants sagged around his waist. He had a wild animal look in his eyes. He staggered towards me, and I cried out, "Mr. Lewis please don't touch me. What are you doing?" He stammered, "I just want to have a little fun. You're very pretty." He grabbed me and pushed me back on the bed. I screamed, "no Mr. Lewis, please let me go. No, no." His big hands held me down on the bed. He uttered, "ah...come on girl. Give Mr. Lewis a little kiss. I won't hurt you, I promise." I pushed him off of me and tried to run out the door. He grabbed my dress and ripped it of my body. He pushed me down on the floor. I stared into his red swollen eyes. His big wed lips touched my face. "Come on, stop fighting me. There is no one here but you and me. I ain't gonna hurt you, Mag." His face was very close to me. I could feel the stubby hairs on his chin. Mr. Lewis unzipped his pants and pulled out his penis. He tried to push my legs apart. I locked my legs together and prayed, "God, please don't let this happen to me."

The strangest thing happened. At that very second, the feeling of power entered my body. I picked up the ashtray from the floor and hammered Mr. Lewis on the head. That didn't stop him. He continued to tear off my bra and rubbing my breast with his rough hands. Time was running out, I thought. I had to do something and to do fast. I lifted my legs up and kicked him hard his balls. He grabbed himself with both hands and I crawled away. He yelled, "you little black bitch. I'll kill you for this."

CHAPTER 3

"THE MYSTERIOUS KILLING"

I ran from the bedroom. All my clothes were torn off except my underpants. The stairs appeared very high. Tears blinded my sight and I slipped on a wine bottle Mr. Lewis had left on the stairway. When I regained conscious, a policeman was lifting me up from the floor. Blood poured from the side of my head. The policeman wrapped a sheet around me.

I pointed upstairs and in a low volume voice I whispered, "where is Mr. Lewis? He...he tried to...to rape me." The policeman didn't say a word. They helped me outside. On my way out of the door I noticed Mr. Lewis' body on the floor covered with a blanket. I rubbed my eyes. This can't be, I thought. The blanket looked like the one my grandfather had. I pinched myself just to make sure I wasn't dreaming. The police picked up an old gun off the floor. I stared at the gun with unbelieving eyes. I watched them placed the gun inside their car. The policeman stopped beside me with a vast look in his eyes. He asked, "do you know whose gun that is?" Whoever owns that gun is the murdered.

I glanced around at Mr. Lewis' body. The blanket disappeared right before my eyes. The policeman ordered me to sit in the car. I watched them through the window. My head was spinning from the fall down stairs. I heard him say, "where 's the blanket?" Both officers looked around the room.

One of the officer murmured, "something strange is going on here. Go check the trunk of the car." He rushed back shouting, "the gun is gone, too."

I sat in the car and my body was shaking from the cold wind. After everything that happened, it was hard for me to believe Mr. Lewis was dead. I wanted to go home. The policeman pulled me out of the car and said, "now look Girl, we are not blaming you for any of this. We need the gun and the blanket for evidence. Do you hear me?" I forced a word from my dry lips. "I'm sorry. I didn't take them. Maybe they were never there." The policeman yelled, "don't talk stupid to us, Girl. We saw the blanket on the body and I put the gun in the trunk myself." He continued, "that man on the floor was shot in the back of his head. We know this was no accident." I braced a smile on my face. Neither was my grandfather's death, I thought. The ambulance took Mr. Lewis body away.

They couldn't call my grandmother because we didn't have a phone. The policemen took me home. Grandma was waiting for me. I jumped out of the car and ran to her crying, "Grandma, Mr. Lewis is dead and he tried to rape me." Grandma yelled, "rape...that low down dirty dog." "He lied to me about his wife being sick. I uttered. No one was home but Mr. Lewis." "I saw grandfather's old blanket covering Mr. Lewis' body, and I recognized the gun, too. It belong to grandfather." Grandma squeezed me close to her, "be quite, girl." "You don't know what you are talking about." She wiped the blood from my face with her dress. She murmured, "thank you Jesus for protecting my baby."

The policemen talked to my grandmother in private. They finally left the farm after asking my grandmother about Mr. Lewis. Grandma came inside with a worried look on her face. I revealed everything that happened to me. She walked into grandfather's room and pulled out his old Bible. She held it close to her heart and she uttered, "thank you Jake for watching over her today." I laid my head on the bed and prayed with Grandma.

There was no evidence and without the gun the case was closed. Nothing else was said to us about what had occurred. I believe the mystery at the scene left the policemen too baffled to explain.

The cold winter went by very fast. I spent most of my time helping my grandmother piece quilts and baking for the church. I won first place with my peanut butter cookies. I was thrilled to complete with the grown-ups. I was only fifteen years old, but my manner displayed an older attitude. I have always lived with older people, and it's easy to pick up their habits.

We didn't go to school during the winter months. School was beginning within the next couple of months. I was excited about going back to school. The school had moved to a new location, which was a little closer to my house. My grandmother had made me several new dresses for school because she didn't care much for me wearing pants. She had stated many times that "it's not ladylike to wear any type of garments that belong to a man." I often wondered if I had worn a pair of blue jeans the day Mr. Lewis tried to rape me, would he have been able to tear them off the way he tore off my dress?

CHAPTER 4

"THE DEATH OF MY BEST FRIEND"

A new family moved into the Lewis' house and the death was left unsolved. The policemen believed that someone else was there with me. Mrs. Lewis revealed to the reporters about the fights she had with her husband and the alcohol abuse she endured daily. She also stated that is why she had left the farm with her children. I will never forget the day Mr. Lewis tried to rape me, nor will I forget the friendship I bonded with his children.

A big truck moved the new family in from Chicago. I wanted to go over and meet the new family, but my grandmother would not allow me to go. Their babysitter, Mrs. Lizzie had moved with them and she had a daughter named Kim. I met Kim the following week and we became very close friends. We were in the same grade. She appeared to be very mature for her age, and I was surprised at some of the things she unveiled to me about herself. Kim wore her hair in a beautiful cut. Her make-up looked really great. I felt so young and plain around her. She came over to my house and showed me how to apply my make-up. Kim combed my hair in a new fashion style, which made me look three of four ears older. I loved it, but my grandmother hated the way I looked. One evening Kim came over and I noticed her breasts were a lot larger. She giggle, "girl, you have so much to learn." She pulled the tissue from her bra and said, "see, this is how you do it." She demonstrated her enlargement tips. Kim reached out to stuff my bra with tissue and said, "girl your breasts are too flat. You need something to fill those flat cups." I laughed at her and refused her method of making the breast larger. Kim filled me in about her boyfriend back home and how much she missed him. I was surprised at some of the things she revealed to me, such as her sexual experiences with older guys when she was only twelve. My grandmother didn't approve of the way Kim dressed, but still she liked her a lot.

Winter passed. There was a new girl in town. Kim attracted all the attention. Everyone wanted to meet her especially all the boys in school. I was happy to be her friend. Maybe, I trusted her a little too much and we went everywhere together. I didn't miss my grandfather as much with Kim as my friend. One day Kim came over to my house. She wore some hot pants so tight that she could barely sit down. I didn't understand why she had to show all of her body. All eyes always fell on her whenever she entered a classroom or walked down the hall. Kim's father was in prison for murdering a police officer. He was sentenced to thirty-five years. Kim talked about her father a lot and each time a worried expression showed on her face.

Kim's mother only finished the fourth grade. She had worked for the Jones family all her life as a maid. Kim always had a lot of money when she came to school. Sometimes she would buy my lunch. I often wondered how she could possible earn so much money. One morning she stepped upon the bus with a black eye. She claimed she had fallen on the steps. I believed her because I no reason not to. Shortly after that, she began missing days from school. Finally, she came over to my house. She had loss weight and dark circles shadowed her thin face. I asked, "Kim, are you okay? What happened to your face?" She pulled a cigarette out of her purse and said, "do you have a light?" My eyes widen in shock. "What, I didn't know you smoked." Kim giggled, "Maggie, there are many things you don't know about me. Well, it's good that you don't." "Kim, is everything okay?" "Yeah, I am fine Maggie. Why are you staring at me?" "Oh...no reason," I replied.

I began to worry about her. She was not the same person. I couldn't believe how different she appeared in just a couple of weeks. I spoke to my grandmother about Kim. She replied, "maybe she is using drugs. You know that stuff will take you down over night." I responded, "no Grandma, that's not true." But in the back of my mind I wasn't sure. As time passed, Kim completely dropped out of school. Three months later, Kim committed suicide. She was five months pregnant. She had taken an overdose of her mother's prescription for diabetes. Kim's mother found her body in bed when she returned from work. We never really knew who the father of her unborn baby was. The rumors spread around the school that she was pregnant by Mr. Jones. Kim's mother worked for the Jones family and Mr. Jones gave Kim money. That's why she always had money in her purse. I was her best friend and she had never spoken to me about her problem. I am so sorry about what happened to her. She deserved a lot more from life.

The day Kim was buried, all the students came to pay their last respects. Kim's mother cried out, "Kim, I tried to warn you, but you wouldn't listen to me." I cried in silence for my friend. My grandmother wrapped her arms around Mrs. Lizzie. She whispered, "go ahead and cry, honey. That's what I did when Jake died."

Kim didn't tell anyone about her pregnancy nor could she live with the secret. I miss her very much. We had lots of fun together. Kim's mother moved out of the Jones' maidservant quarters. The Jones sold the farm and moved back to Chicago.

CHAPTER 5

"FIRST LOVE"

Five years have passed since my grandfather died. I am a freshman in college. I work part-time at the Rice factory. The work is very hard and the hours are long. I know God will keep me strong in spirit to go on. I have to work twice as hard because I am a woman and a black woman too. My grandfather taught me a long time ago, "if you are going to do a job, put all your efforts in doing it right." He would say, "the harder you work, girl, the luckier you'll get." My grandparents helped me to understand that you can love someone and still not like the way they present themselves.

Going to college and working every night is hard for me. I am not home very much to help my grandmother around the house. I notice her sometimes and she seems so tired. Her hair is completely gray and her face shows sign of aging. Once I came home from work late and my grandmother was not in her room. I checked the kitchen for her. I wondered where could she be at this late hour. I glanced out the window. Grandma was standing over my grandfather's grave. She was talking to him as if he was standing there with her. I noticed the peculiar look on her face and I embraced her. She never stop talking. She stared at me with tears in her eyes. She murmured, "Jake, I miss you so much. Soon we will be together again." "Grandma come back inside," I cried.

I helped her back to bed and she fell asleep immediately. I observed her as she slept, thinking to myself, what would life be without her." She had explained to me one day, "Maggie, when I die bury me beside Jake...not at his feet or his head, but right beside him. What a strange thing for my grandmother to request, I thought. I realized she would die one day. I prayed that she would be around a little longer with me. I don't want to think about death. Especially, my grandmother leaving me alone on this earth...it is too depressing. I have a lot more to engage my mind with.

I met this wonderful guy on my job. His name is Dan Forrest. His smile reminded me of a little boy. We talked on our lunch break everyday. I invited him over to meet my grandmother. Grandma went out of her way to make that day special for me. She cleaned and baked all day. When Dan arrived late that evening, Grandma was so tired she excused herself to her room.

Dan and I talked after dinner. He asked questions about the farm and me. Dan had moved here from Memphis to be close to his mother. We strolled around the farm and I showed him where my grandfather was buried. Dan took my hands and replied, "girl, you are something else. One of these days I am going to make you my wife." "Is he serious?" I thought. He stared at me with those big brown eyes while waiting for my response. I held my breath while excitement raced through my body. Could this really happen to me? Dan gave me a big hug. "How do you feel about that?" I blabbered, "I have always wanted to get married. You know, settle down with a wonderful man. Oh yeah, and have a couple of kids." He kissed me lightly on the cheek. "Me too," he replied.

Dan asked if we were thinking about selling the farm now that my grandfather was dead. The conversation between Dan and me began to focus on the welfare of the farm. The questions he asked, made me wonder...why is he so interested in the farm?" Dan lived about three miles from me. He admired my grandfather's picture on the wall. He reacted, "wow, he was a big man." I heard that your grandfather had an accident in the woods. He fell and shot himself in the head. I responded, "no, Grandpa was killed. Mr. Lewis and his friends were in the woods the day my grandfather was shot." Dan asked, "how are you so sure about that?" I uttered, "you never mind, I am sure."

Dan smiled with a peculiar flare in his eyes. He pulled me into his powerful arms and kissed me on the lips. His body pressed hard, making my body explode with desires. I pushed Dan away..."no, it's too soon for this. I think you better go no." Dan didn't want to leave, but I insisted. He left quickly as he kissed me on the cheeks. Wow! What a feeling, I thought.

I looked in on my grandmother and she was sound asleep. I kissed her goodnight. Later, I heard the dogs barking and wondered why they were barking. I peeped out of the window. It was strange, the dogs only barked when someone came to the farm. I watched the dogs for a few seconds. Maybe, they were barking at the moon.

I laid in bed thinking about the way Dan kissed me. The next day I rushed to work. Dan was waiting for me at the water fountain. He touched my hand, "hello, I am glad you could make it. How is your grandmother today?" "I can't afford to miss work. My grandmother is feeling better." The main reason was because I didn't want to miss seeing Dan's face, I thought. I am falling in love with him. Maybe, he will marry me. I grinned with a big smile on my face.

Dan and I dated for eight months. We saw each other everyday. One day when he came over Grandma was in the garden, and we had the whole house to ourselves. Dan kissed me and I didn't want him to stop. I clinged to him as he pulled me closer. "Maggie, I need you, please say you will marry me one day." My heart was pounding rapidly. I answered, "yes, I will marry you." Dan pushed me back on the sofa and his hands were all over my body. He pulled my dress up and caressed my thighs. My whole body was burning with desire. He unzipped his pants and placed my hand on his penis. Wow! His penis felt like a hard rock. I wanted him and I didn't want him to stop. Grandma, please stay in the garden a little longer, I thought as we made love on the sofa.

Finally my grandmother came inside. She observed me with a big question on her mind. She uttered, "Maggie, you sure have been seeing a lot of that boy, Dan. I hope you are taking time and not rushing into anything too fast." She gazed around the room. Now you know, a man will do or say anything to get what he wants." She paused for a second...her eyes glanced over the room. She continued, "after that, he's off for the next easy catch." I focused my eyes away from my grandmother, knowing how wise and knowledgeable she was. I was guilty. I was the easy catch. I was so caught up in a moment of passion and the thought of using protection never entered my mind. My thoughts were preoccupied. I forgot Grandma was speaking to me. She shouted, "Maggie Johnson, do you hear me talking to you?" I jumped nearly out of my skin. She shook her head and waved her hand in the air. "Girl, what are you thinking about so hard?" I smiled, "oh Grandma, I am just thinking about all the homework I have to do before tomorrow." Grandma stared at me as if she knew I was lying. "You young people are so hard to understand."

Several weeks passed and I saw Dan everyday at work. He didn't say anything else about marrying me. I loved Dan. I decided to wait until he was ready to make the big step. Dan didn't like for me to nag him about things. My cycle was two weeks late and I was so nervous. Finally, it did show. We were very careful after that first mistake. Dan didn't like the idea of using a condom when we made love. I insisted that he use one or he wouldn't see any action at all. One Sunday after church, Dan came over for dinner. We talked about our future together. He wanted to know that if I had any more relatives living close by. He inquired, "who would become the owner if something should happed to your grandmother. Dan kissed me. He continued, "what would you do with this big farm?" I grinned, "I can handle the farm if I had to." Dan folded his arms. "Well, I am thinking ahead of time. You know your grandmother is up in age and she is sick all the time.

We kissed good night and Dan left early. He didn't go the same direction he normally take when he went home. Instead, he took the back road behind the farm. I wondered why he decided to go that direction home. Taking the back road took almost twice the time to go home. The only thing back there were my grandfather's cows and an old barn filled with hay. The next day I asked Dan why he went home the back way. He retained, "well, I wanted to see how large the farm really was. My grandmother owned about 400 acres of land covered mostly with trees. My grandmother had informed me that whenever she died the farm and everything would belong to me. I didn't want Dan to know that because his conversation would always end up inquiring about the farm.

CHAPTER 6

"CROSSING OVER ON THE OTHER SIDE"

My grandmother's health was declining each day. She lost a lot of weight. Her thin body moved around very slow. One evening Dan came over to see me and Grandma was sitting in a chair. Dan asked, "how you feeling, Mrs. Johnson?" She never answered him. She held her head down without a word. Dan glanced at me; "she's not feeling well today." With a sad tone in my voice, I murmured, "no she's not doing very well today." I helped her back to bed. Sometimes she would stay in bed all day and forget to take her medication. The medicines were for her enlarged heart. Without it, she could have major heart attacks.

I stayed home from school for a week. One night Grandma called me into her room. She had a strange look in her eyes. I knew something was wrong. She whispered, "Maggie, Jake is waiting for me. I am ready to go now," she smiled. "I am not going to be here with you too much longer." I fell down on my knees and cried. "No Grandma, please don't talk like that." She touched my face and said, "Maggie, I love you very much. You will never be alone. Do the best you can and God will stay by your side. He won't leave you." Tears began to flow down my Grandmother's face. Her voice faded to a whisper. She rested her head backward on the pillow with her eyes staring at the ceiling. Her breathing became very shallowed. I begged, "Grandma, please let me take you to the hospital." She touched my arm. "There's no need for you to take me to the hospital, I know its time for me to go. Don't cry anymore. Wipe those tears away. Be happy for me." She panted, "I love you, take care of yourself." She took a deep breath and turned her head towards my grandfather's grave. She murmured her last words. "Jake, I am ready to join you."

I couldn't believe my grandmother was dead. The room became very calm. I looked around the bedroom and the door slowly opened. I saw my grandfather standing in the doorway with the old blanket in his hand. He appeared at the foot of her bed and covered my grandmother's body with the blanket. I touched the blanket and my grandfather vanished before my eyes. I was not afraid of my grandfather, for I knew his spirit lived on the farm. I called for the ambulance and my cousin. I went back into the bedroom. The blanket covering my grandmother's body was gone. She laid in bed with a peaceful look on her face. I held her hand until I heard a knock at the door. The medical team were here to take my grandmother's body away. When they left, I fell down on the bed and cried. "Oh God, help me."

We buried my grandmother besides my grandfather. During the funeral I waited for my grandfather to appear again, but he never did. Three months after my grandmother's death, I was trying to get my life back on track. I thought about selling the farm. There were so much to do. I really didn't want to move away. It was Dan who suggested that I sell the farm. Dan was by my side every minute after my grandmother died. He even spent weekends over to help me on the farm. One day I came home from school and Dan was there probing through some important papers. When he noticed me, he seemed very surprised. He advised me that he was just concerned about my welfare. He wanted to make sure I was able to take care of everything. I warned Dan about going through my personal belongings. Dan said he was sorry, and that he didn't mean anything by it.

I cooked supper for us and Dan sat at the table and read the newspaper. After we ate, we talked for awhile. He took my hand and said, "I am worried about you living out here all alone. Maybe, it's time we get married. He asked, do you need more time to think about it?" I answer, "no, I think I've waited long enough." Dan pulled me up from my chair and kissed me. He promised, "you won't be alone anymore, Maggie. I will take good care of you."

Dan and I were married on Christmas day. I wished my grandparents were alive to be here. The wedding was very simple, and we invited only a few people to the wedding. Dan's mother and father were there. Only a handful of people from the mill factory attended. Mrs. Carter baked me a large wedding cake with six layers. People from the church brought gifts and large plates of food. We said our vows and kissed. Everything was over quickly and I was glad when all the guests left. Dan used his father's car. We boarded a bus to Memphis, TN that night. Dan didn't feel up to driving, so we enjoyed the ride together. We visited some of the nice clubs and danced late into the night. Dan noticed the attention I was drawing from the guys in the club, because all the fellows were eyeing me. I will never forget the feeling I experienced.

Later we relaxed in our room and Dan ordered wine. I laid down on the big king-size bed. Dan stared at me and said, "you are so beautiful. I am a very lucky man to marry a woman like you." We kissed and I melted in Dan's arms. "I love you," I whispered. He smiled, "I love you too, Sweetheart.

"I'm going to take a quick shower, " I uttered. Dan pulled me closer to him and kissed me behind the ear. I murmured, "let me go freshen up for you. I will only take a minute." He replied, "okay Darling, I hope you won't take too long." I grabbed my overnight bag and hurried into the bathroom. I took a hot shower and slipped into my beautiful black gown. I was admiring myself in the mirror as I dabbed a little sexy perfume behind my ears. I was a beautiful black woman. Dan was lucky to have me as his wife. When I came out of the bathroom, Dan had fixed me a drink. I took a couple of sips from my glass. Dan began kissing me and we made love all night long, while the music on the radio played low.

I woke up the next morning in Dan's arms. He beamed, "good morning, Mrs. Forrest. Would you like some breakfast?" I uttered, "oh no, I have a splitting headache." I took two aspirins and we stayed in bed most of the day. Finally, we dressed and went out to eat later that evening. I was very happy. I stared at the beautiful wedding band Dan had given me. We had a lovely dinner together, and afterward we visited a musical Theatre. We had a wonderful honeymoon. The time passed quickly.

We took a late train back home. The next morning there was lots of work to keep us busy. Dan feed the cows, and I gathered the eggs and feed the dogs. I also checked the mailbox. I peeped over at my grandparents' grave. Even though I was happy, the absence of my grandparents generated sadness in my heart. I wish my grandmother were here with me. There are so many things I wanted to share with her. We would always talk before going to bed every night. She helped me to understand the true meaning of caring and respecting others. As I flipped through the mail, I noticed a letter from a real estate agent. The letter was addressed to Dan Forrest. Maybe he was trying to get a job with one of the real estate companies, I thought. As I stared at the address on the letter I thought, he did take a class in real estate. I placed the mail on the table.

Dan came in later after feeding the cows. He suggested hiring someone to help out on the farm. He didn't like feeding the cows. The work was too much for one person to keep up with, he stated. Dan had already made up his mind. The next day he hired Mrs. Carter's oldest son, Tim. Things worked out between Dan and Tim. Tim was a hard working person and he didn't mind working late hours.

We know what a person thinks not when he tells us what he thinks by his actions.

I.B.S.

CHAPTER 7

"FACES OF DECEPTION"

Dan and I have been married for three years and many things have changed. We brought a new car, painted the house and put in new windows. Yet, there are no children. Oh yes, Dan sold my grandfather's cows. I was very upset because he didn't tell me anything until after he had sold them. He said, he had discussed it with me, that I just didn't remember. No, I don't think I would forget anything of that nature. I wanted to know what happened to the money. I opened up the subject about the letter from the real estate. He tried to convince me there was no letter. However, I knew Dan was lying. I saw the letter myself and wondered why would he conceal the truth about it.

Dan seemed so different. He was definitely not the same man I married. I began to worry about him. Maybe, he was sick and not telling me. The next morning at breakfast, I asked, "Dan are you okay?" He glanced at me as he sipped his coffee. "I am fine, why do you ask?" "Well, we need to talk because there are some things I am not please with," I uttered. Dan's expression changed and he reacted by saying, "you want to know what happened to the money. Well, how do you think we purchased that car in the driveway." He pushed away from the table. He continued with a mask look on his face, "I paid other bills, too." He replied, "I sold the cows because we needed the money."

Dan was hiding something. From that day forward, I didn't trust him anymore. I became more involved with the function of running the farm. We didn't need to sell the cows. My grandmother had left me a large sum of money from her life insurance policy. I asked questions about things and about every mistake that was made. Dan was not pleased with my new attitude. His habits changed. He began to go out and come home very late. One night he came home very drunk. When I opened the door, he fell on the floor. His face and hands were covered with mud. He blabbered, "Maggie, the car is in the ditch. I lost control of it because the roads are slippery. "Now Maggie, don't start nagging me. You know when it rain, these roads are like a sliding board." I stepped away from the door, and left Dan lying on the floor looking foolish. He uttered, "Honey, we can use the tractor and pull the car home tomorrow. I don't think anyone will try to steal it."

Without another word to Dan, I went to bed and alone. I didn't want to argue with him. The next day Dan and Tim pulled the car out of the ditch. I was very disappointed with Dan. Everytime I looked at him I wanted to scream. I noticed sometimes that I felt stressed out. My head ached all the time and I was losing weight and looking tired. My first thought was that maybe I was pregnant. I made an appointment to see the doctor. I was so sure I was pregnant, but the doctor told me that my test was negative. I asked him to test me again to be sure. The doctor explained that I was under a lot of stress. He said that I was in good health, but needed to take some vitamins and iron tablets. Maybe, they would even help me to get pregnant quicker. I thanked him and took the prescriptions. He also gave me a prescription to help me sleep. I really don't know why I couldn't sleep at night. Maybe, it was because Dan was always out late.

I explained to Dan what the doctor had said about the medication helping me to become pregnant. Dan shocked me by saying, "well, I am not ready for kids right now. I prefer to wait a couple more years." I was too tired to discuss it anymore with him. We have been married for almost four years and he is still not ready for kids. I took my medicine and went to bed and it worked right away. I fell asleep within minutes. I was already asleep when Dan came in to bed.

The next day I was cleaning up in the living room and noticed that Dan had been looking over the deeds and other papers to the farm. When Dan came home that night, I asked him about the papers. He told me I should have his name on the deeds and insurance papers because he was my husband. I really didn't want to fuss with Dan about this matter. I know we should share things together. I didn't trust him anymore.

Dan talked me into adding his name to the deeds. We went down town the next week and changed the papers. I had wanted to talk to someone about the matter, so I visited Mrs. Carter. I informed her about Dan's drinking and staying out late at night. She was very understanding. She searched my face over with her big brown eyes. She uttered, "Maggie, you and Dan have been married for four years. Where are the kids?" I revealed my visit to the doctor and the medicine I was taking. She nodded her head and folded her arms. "Now, you say you are not taking anything to prevent you from getting pregnant. Well, it must be Dan. He should be checked out, too." We talked for a long time. I also advised her about adding Dan's name to the deeds and she reacted by asking, whose idea was that? I unveiled how Dan insisted that I add his name to the deeds because he was my husband. Mrs. Carter pulled herself up from her chair and said, "girl, if your grandfather could see this, Dan would have a fight on his hands...transferring that land into another man's name." Mrs. Carter had made her point. I thanked her for the water as I walked towards the door. She touched me on the shoulder with a twinkle in her eye. "I wish you good luck. You be careful and don't forget to come back and visit me again."

I drove back to the farm. Dan was sitting at the table. He looked up as I opened the door and angrily asked, "now where in the hell have you been all day? I wanted to use the car." I hunged up my coat and looked over the mail on the table. His voice sounded irritated and he pushed away from the table and knocked a glass on the floor. He blurted out, "Mag, why don't we sell the farm and move to town. I am tired of this whole damn thing." I yelled, "no, I will not sell this farm. How could you asked me that?" I picked up the broken glass. I warned Dan, "if you are tired of living on the farm, well, you can pack up your damn things and leave."

From that day forward, Dan avoided talking to me about anything. He would sleep on the couch or watch TV all night.

I realized my marriage was falling apart. Several months passed and we didn't talked about selling the farm. One night after I took my shower and prepared to go to bed, Dan raised up off the sofa and said, "Mag, don't forget to take your medicine." I went to the bathroom to get my pills and realized I didn't have any more. I pretended to be asleep when Dan came to bed. Dan lay there for a few minutes. He made sure I was sound asleep. Finally, he got up slowly trying not to disturb me. I laid there quietly, faking a snoring sound. Dan was convinced I had taken my medicine and would sleep for a while. I waited until he left the room. I could hear him tossing paper in the trash can. I slowly moved from my bed and peeped through the door. Dan was sitting at the desk writing something over and over. I didn't want him to see me, so I tipped back to bed. I wondered all night long what Dan was up to.

The next day after Dan left for work, I checked the trash can in the living room. He had taken the trash to the dumpster out back. Dan was up to something, I thought. I was going to find out what. I rushed out to the back porch and pulled out the garage bag. There were several torn pieces of paper with my name on it. I was angry. My hands were shaking. I sat down on the ground and matched the torn pieces of paper together. Dan was practicing writing my name for only one reason. He was going to forge my signature and sell the farm. I didn't want to believe this was happening to me. Tears clouded my eyes. How could he do this to me?

Was this Dan's plan from the very beginning?" I didn't hear the car pull up in the driveway. I raised up quickly. Dan was standing in the doorway. He uttered, "you look like hell tonight. What is your problem?" I held up the pieces of papers. "This is my damn problem, you got some explaining to do." He responded, "What got your feathers all blown up? You must be on your period. That how you all get." Without blinking an eye, I yelled, "why are you practicing signing my name?" He walked away from me. I screamed, "Dan Forrest, you better tell me the truth?" Dan finished drinking his beer and stepped towards the door. I grabbed his arm and he pushed me away. He shouted, "look I don't want you nagging me tonight about no damn pieces of paper. I don't know anything about it." I screamed at him again, "you lying bastard." Dan slapped me hard across my face. "Shut your damn mouth." He knocked the papers out of my hand. He boasted, "" see you have been searching the trash can. You just can't leave things alone, can you Mag?"

He stunned me by his reaction, but it did not surprise me. I wiped the blood from my nose. I was afraid because this was not the same man I had married. I knew something terrible was going to happen. Dan had never acted like this before with me. I motioned to leave the room, but Dan knocked me back on the floor. He pulled my hair back from my face and grinned down at me, "well Girl, I guess it's time you learned the truth. You see I found someone to buy the farm. There is only one small problem." He picked up the pieces of paper off the floor. "I can't get your signature, right? I have been practicing for awhile. Now, are you ready to sign these paper?" I jumped up and ran out the door and Dan was right behind me. I tripped over a stick on the ground. Dan laughed, "now, where are you going, my dear sweet wife?" He pulled me back inside and tied my hands together with a rope.

Dan opened the cabinet door and pulled out a brown bag. He was eyeing me like a criminal. I couldn't believe my eyes. There were thousands of dollars in the bag. Dan bragged, "I have been saving for this day. The money I got from selling your grandfather's cows is right here in this bag. I hate to do this to you, Baby, but you wouldn't go alone with my idea to sell this farm." Dan played with the rings on my finger. He smiled, "it was wonderful while it lasted, Maggie. But, I have better things I want to do with my life. All you want to do is work and raise a family." I put my head on the floor and prayed, "Oh God, please help me. Don't let him kill me." Dan looked down at me. "No" let me see. You know why you can't get pregnant? My dear lady, I had a vasectomy a long time ago. I can't have kids and I never wanted to have any with you."

I sit there and listened to Dan's conversation, knowing it was the truth. I wondered how could I have been so stupid. Dan never wanted to talk about having children. I begged Dan to let me go. He pulled me upon my feet and pushed me out the door. I cried out, "Dan, where are you taking me?" He didn't answer. We passed my grandparents' graves I prayed that someone would save me. I wondered where Tim was. Maybe, he would come over. Dan picked up the shovel from the rack on the barn door. I thought, what is he going to do? We walked behind the barn. I noticed a big hole in the ground. My God, he had already dug a grave for me. My heart stopped beating. I froze in my tracks. My legs were weak. I tried to run, but with my hands tied behind me I couldn't get very far. I fell to the ground and my lips were bleeding and my knees were hurt badly. All I could think about at that moment was to try to get away from Dan. I tried to pull my hands free. The wet rope was too tight. The more I struggled, the rope cut deeper into my flesh. Dan placed the shovel on the ground. He pranced over to me with a foolish grin on his face. Why, Maggie, no one will ever find you out here. They will just think you are away on another trip."

I laid on the cold ground and closed my eyes. There was nothing I could do. Dan kneeled down and kissed me. He fingered my breasts as he unzipped his pants. He took out his penis, and with a silly grin, he uttered, "I might as well enjoy this one more time. I must say, I really did enjoy it a lots." When he finished he zipped up his pants. He nodded, "let's get on with the show." I pleaded with him again to let me go. I blabbed out, "I will sell the farm. Please, I will sign the papers." Dan grinned at me, "oh, Honey, you're just saying that because you are afraid of what I am going to do to you." I pulled at Dan's pant leg. He slapped me across my face and said, "lay down and put your face to the ground. I don't want you looking at." I screamed, no! I want you to look me in the eyes. I hope you will never forget what you are about to do. How could you do this to me?" Dan stepped closer to me with the shovel in his hand...ready to strike me. At that very moment I saw a bright light from a distance. I rubbed my eyes. The light came closer to Dan. I put my hand over my mouth and took a deep breath. A figure appeared in the light. What is this, I thought. It looks like the shape of a man's face. I jumped up and ran. When I looked back, I saw my grandfather's old blanket floating in mid-air approaching Dan. The blanket wrapped around Dan's neck and pulled his body up into the tree. Dan kicked and screamed out for me to help him. I watched Dan's body hang limp from the branch. He was dead. I felt the rope loosen from my wrists. I understood what was happening. I wasn't afraid anymore. My grandfather's spirit had returned to protect me. I started walking back to the farm. My body was tired. I looked back. Dan's body laid limp on the ground under the tree. The blanket was no longer there. As I passed my grandfather's grave, I whispered, "thank you, Grandpa for saving my life again."

◆

CHAPTER 8

"WHO KILLED DAN FOREST"

As I staggered back to the farm, my heart was rapidly beating. The picture of Dan hanging from the branch focused in my mind. My legs were trembling. I fell down on the ground. What am I going to do. Dan is dead. "Stay calm Maggie, I thought. Don't panic and call the police." The ambulance and the police arrived on the scene. I explained what had happened. He wrote down my statement, not missing a word. The policemen asked me to show them where the body was. I led them to the spot where Dan had been killed. His limp body laid on the ground under the big oak tree. The police asked me again, "how did you say this happened?" They stared at me with curious eyes. I nervously uttered, "Dan's body was pulled up in the tree by a bright light shaped like a blanket."

The police related to each other in a very muted voice. One of them swiftly stepped towards me and spoke in an authoritative tone of voice. "Miss, anything you say or do can be used against you in a court of law. Do you understand me?" My voice quiver as I answered, "yes, I ...ugh...I understand, but...what do you mean? Ugh...ugh...do you think I killed him? No, no, I didn't kill him." The policemen watched me with a weird look on their face. I uttered, "the blanket...ugh...ugh, it...appeared in this spot." The police eyeballed each other, "what blanket? Miss, we don't want to hear anything about a dawn blanket. All we want to know was anyone else in the woods with you and your husband." I murmured, "no Sir." I was trying to hold back my tears. The policemen requested, "well, you have some explaining to do." He pulled Dan's hair apart to expose the big gushy wound in his head. "You see Miss, this man was shot in the back of the head." The other officer leaned against the tree and he pointed at the wound in Dan's head. He reacted, "wow!" That looks like a nasty shotgun wound. I glanced quickly at Dan's head. A shiver of fear speared through me. There was a huge bloody hole in the back of Dan's head. I couldn't bare the sight of it. I screamed, "no, no, I didn't kill him...it wasn't me. My grandfather did it. The police hesitated. "Oh, I thought you said that you and your husband were the only ones in the woods. This wasn't an accident. Your husband was murder...were you trying to kill him or did the gun just go off in your hand?" I slowly arched down on the ground. Tears flowed down my cheeks. I pleaded, "no I didn't kill him. I don't own a gun. Dan tried to kill me. He wanted to sale the farm, but I wouldn't sign the papers...so he plotted to kill me. I pointed toward the hole Dan had dug. "See that hole in the ground. His intention was to bury me in that grave. I blabbered, "I can't explain what happened here last night. A supernatural thing occurred. You see my grandfather is dead, but his spirit still exists. He protects me from any harm.

The police gloated at me as if I was speaking another language. He retorted, "lady, are you on some type of drugs because what you are telling us sound like something from the twilight zone. You need to come with us." They dragged me upon my feet. "We're taking you in for more questions." The paramedic placed Dan's body inside the ambulance. The police led me towards their car. I stop quickly in my track. "Please, Sir, may I get my coat?" The officer shouted, "hurry up Miss. We have other things to take care of."

I hurried into the house and pulled opened the closet door. There before my eyes appeared my grandfather holding his old gun. I shouted, "oh my God, you are here." The police heard me screaming. They rushed into the room. One of the officer yelled furiously, "what's wrong lady? We heard you yell." I nervously replied, "oh nothing. I hit my head on the door." The officer uttered, "be careful, we don't want anything else happening out here in these woods. You are the only witness we have." I pulled my coat off the hanger. My eyes searched the room for my grandfather. I peeped around the door. He's here, I thought to myself.

As we drove away from the farm, I glanced back for one last glimpse of the farm. All the lights were on in the house. I remember turning off the lights before I left. I was stunned and speechless. I focused my eyes on the farm. All the rooms were lit up with a brilliance ray of colors. I quickly glanced around at the officers. They were so busy smoking and talking about me making up the whole thing. They paid no attention to the unnatural aurora of lights. I began to wonder what was my grandfather up to now. I was sure he would help me, but I didn't really know how. I thought, I didn't want him to kill anyone else again. I tapped on the glass window between us. The police looked back with a frown on his face. He uttered, "what in the hell do you want now?" I begged, with a quiver in my voice. "Please don't take me to jail. I want to go home. You are making a big mistake. My grandfather is angry." The officers busted out laughing. One of the officer imitated me..."grandfather is angry." "Grandfather is angry." He pointed a finger at me, "look you crazy woman, your grandfather is dead." We are placing you under arrest." You need to be locked up in the cuckoo house. I angrily shouted with fear in my voice, "he won't let you harm me or put me in jail. The police demanded me to be quiet, or they would tape my mouth close.

I put my head down in my lap and prayed. After about five minutes the car came to an abrupt stop. I sat up not knowing what was happening. The ambulance was parked on the side of the road with the doors opened. The driver was sitting there starring at his hands. The police pulled up beside the ambulance and called the paramedic by name. There were no responds from him. I focused my eyes on the front seat. My grandfather was sitting between the two officers. Suddenly, their faces showed a blank expression. Without saying a word, they turned around and headed back toward the farm. The ambulance followed the police car. They acted like zombies, as if they were under a spell. They speeded down the country road. I glanced up and my grandfather was still sitting there. I covered my eyes and screamed, "Grandpa, please don't kill them. You must stop this, it's not right."

The car abruptly stopped at the farm. The ambulance speeded towards the woods. One of the officers pulled me out of the car. He took off my handcuffs and quickly hurdled me out of the car. I frantically ran home. They speeded away with an expressionless look on their faces. I locked the doors behind me. They are gone, I thought. I peeped out of the window. Suddenly I felt my grandfather's presence in the house. He appeared again and spoke, "as long as they don't hurt you, they will live. Their minds are completely blank. I took away their memories. They will not remember what occurred here tonight." This was the first time my grandfather had actually talked to me since his death. Although I have seen him many times, I was not afraid. He faded through the door in a ghostly manner. I pulled my coat around my shoulders and braced my body against the door. I thought to myself, many unaccountable things have happened. "My grandfather's spirit can't rest. Why is he still wandering around on this earth? The blanket was never found nor was his gun. Maybe he's trouble by something on this earth."

My head ached from all the turmoil. I took two aspirins for my pain and fell asleep. A knock at the door woke me up. I jumped up quickly lurching to the door. I asked, "who is it?" It was a reporter from Glenville News center. I slowly opened the door, but I was not yet completely awakened. "Yes, what do you want?" The two policemen greeted me, "good morning, miss." The older man replied, "we are here to asked you a few questions about what happened here last night. I rubbed my eyes, "what are you talking about," I responded? The young reporter replied, "miss, we need to know exactly what occurred here. We have three men in the hospital with no memories. We know they came to this farm last night. They responded to a call from someone at this resident. Did you call the police last night, he asked?" "No, you have the wrong place I uttered." "May we come in, he requested?" The reporter glanced around the room. He insisted, "something very mysterious happened which left three men in some type of trance. They have no memory of what happened last night. The older man continued, "you have not been listen to the news?" I reacted with an unsusceptible twist in my voice. "New...ugh...TV...why...no, I just woke up. I really don't understand what you are talking about. The younger reporter asked, "miss, we asked if you know anything about this." I scratched my head; "I just can't remember anything...ugh...ugh...about last night.

I blinked my eyes and rubbed my hands together. I thought for a second, "the reporters would think I am crazy if I explained what happened. Why not pretend I am insane," I thought. The mysterious appearing of my grandfather will be far beyond their human comprehension. I hoped this idea would work. I flashed my eyes from one reporter to another. I paced the floor as they watched me with inquisitive eyes. The reporters appeared a little jittery. I knocked the picture off the wall. I shouted, "my grandfather did it. My grandfather did it." Now you go on leave. I don't know anything at all. Please leave, there is nothing I can tell you." I tossed my hair, shaking my head in a vigorous manner. I scattered clothes all over the place and I hurled my body across the sofa, flipping over the chair. The reporters stared at me. One of them whispered to the other, "she is insane. We better try to leave here in one piece." They scampered out the door and hurdled into their car throwing gravel as they speeded away.

♦

CHAPTER 9

"THE GRAVE"

I busted out laughing at the sight of them running. I couldn't believe I had really pulled it off. I tricked them into believing I was an insane person. Well, they wouldn't believe me if I told them the truth. I was sorry about what happened to the officers. They were going to put me in a jail and throw away the key. I gathered up all the clothes off the floor. As I was picking up the clothes, I noticed a brown bag on the floor. I opened it quickly. The bag was filled with money. I remembered it was the same brown bag Dan had before he dragged me into the woods. I empty the money out on the table and the total amount was three thousand dollars. I wrapped the money up and placed it under my pillow. I thought, Dan Forest you got what you deserved. I fixed myself a hot cup of tea. At that time the phone rang. The voice on the other end was Tim. "Hello Maggie, I am calling to see if Dan needs any help today." I hesitated for a second. Tim, I have some bad news to tell you, Dan is dead. He was killed in a drastic accident last night. Tim sounded shocked to hear the bad news. He wanted to know what happened to Dan. I tried to explain, not really telling the truth about his death. A freak accident caused Dan's death, I said. Tim paused for a second and uttered, "I can't believe this." I quickly changed the conversation before Tim asked me any more questions. Tim was very upset because he respected Dan. He asked in a low trembling voice, "are you okay, Maggie?" I answered, "yes, I am fine."

After the lengthy conversation with Tim, I suddenly remembered the paramedics had returned Dan's body back to the woods. I dashed out the door and grabbed a shovel from the barn. As I approached the woods, I saw the black bag beside the road. I thought, oh, no. I pulled Dan's body back into the woods. Then I remembered Dan had dug a grave for me. His plans backfired on him. I will bury him in his own grave, I thought. I rolled Dan's body over, not wanting to look at the bag. I closed my eyes. Maybe, this was only a dream. Sweat and dirt covered my face. I pushed Dan's stiff body into the shallow grave and used the shovel to cover him. I packed the soil down very tight.

After finishing up, I was sure everything would be all right. I wiped my face with the tail of my skirt. With one foot on Dan's grave, I bid him farewell. I realized what I had done and a nauseated feeling entered into my stomach. I was acting like a person with something to hide. Why did I lie to the reporters? I am confused about everything. I buried Dan's body to protect myself. No one would believe my grandfather had killed Dan. There is no way I could explain this mysterious murder.

I began to sense an errie feeling floating over my body as I walked home. The thought of keeping this a secret for the rest of my life was too overpowering. I feel as if I am living in two worlds. The world of the living and the world of the dead. I have no control over the things that have changed my life. I am afraid of my actions. I sat down on the steps. The farm is quiet and lonely. I can't describe the emotional impact of Dan's death. I placed the shovel inside the barn. Spook, my black cat ran between my legs. My grandfather gave me the cat before he died. I know he cared for me while he was living, but I wish he wouldn't return to this world again. I have no way of explaining the things that he had done. The policemen didn't believe me. They thought I was a lunatic. The death of my husband will haunt me for the rest of my life. A mysterious secret, I thought.

I switched on the television and finally they showed the policemen on the news. Their dull-witted faces showed no expression, not even blinking of an eye. I rushed out the door to my Grandparents' grave. I thought, "Grandpa, please don't do this again. You can't protect me this way. You are making my life miserable. The things you have done to protect me, I can't explain them. On one will believe me. Please, please, Grandpa don't come back again. How can I help your spirit rest? I know you are looking for something, and whatever it is, it means a great deal to you. Why are you wandering around the farm?" I picked up the flower reef and placed them back on top of the grave. I loved my grandfather very much. He was the strength in our family. He took care of us. I turned around to my grandmother's grave. Her spirit has not been seen. She is at peace with this world. I lifted up the flowers on her grave. My grandparents, the two people that I loved more than myself are dead.

I wandered into my grandfather's room. Everything was neatly in place the way my grandmother had left them. I looked inside the closet. There was a large box on the shelf. I opened the box. My grandmother had neatly folded up all of my grandfather's clothes. I carefully looked over all the things. I continued looking through the drawer. There were several pictures of my mother when she was a baby, a bracelet and a small dark arrowhead. I checked under the bed and there was a large chest filled with old newspapers and letters. I quickly sorted through the letters. Several discolored old maps were mixed in with the miscellaneous items. I spread the maps on the bed. One of the maps appeared very familiar to me. What was the map for? There was a big (X) mark on the map in the far right corner. The layout was a map of the woods in the back of the farm. The (X) was marked about four miles from the farm. I thought, "why was the spot marked on the map? What was the meaning of this?" I am sure it was something my grandfather was looking for. He spends a large part of his time in the woods.

I placed all the other items back inside the chest, except the map. I pushed the chest back under the bed. I heard a sound coming from the kitchen. "Who's there," I shouted? Crumbs were scattered on the floor. A chair was turned over. The room commences to feeling cold. The curtain began to move. I felt my legs shaking, fearing the thought of Dan coming back to revenge his death. "Who are you? What do you want?" As my eyes searched the room, suddenly my grandfather appeared in the doorway. The room became an aurora of bright light. He spoke in a deep voice, "look for the big tree in the woods behind the farm." The lights disappeared. I peeped out the window. "What is it about the woods that hold the secrets of the past. My grandfather's spirit will not rest until the woods give up the secrets of his death. Grandpa believed in the recreation of love ones through other people. He told me once that the blanket belonged to his father. I didn't understand the meaning of his words until now. I understand the blanket holds the spirit of my love ones. I feel the spirit of my grandfather working within me.

I cleaned up the mess off the floor and prepared supper for myself. Farm life is lonely, I thought about my honeymoon trip with Dan, which was the last trip away. My life on the farm is like a prison. I can't forget the pain of living alone in this world, without loving somebody. After eating a light supper, I laid down on the sofa and cried myself to sleep.

The next morning I visited the hospital. I wanted to see if the men had regained their memories back. I checked with the front desk nurse. I had hoped to see the men that were admitted to the hospital yesterday. She asked me if I would wait there for a few minutes. She returned shortly with another nurse. The nurse motioned for me to follow her. We walked down the hall to room #244. The nurse opened the door for me and returned to her desk. I couldn't believe my eyes. The policemen laid in the bed with their arms strapped to the beds. Their eyes were gazed at the ceiling. My grandfather did this to these men. I was sadden by the sight. I ran out of the hospital with tears in my eyes. I stopped for a second to get myself together. As I walked towards my car, I noticed Tim Carter leaving the hospital. I asked, "what are you doing at the hospital?" Tim responded that his mother had a stroke last night and she is in the intensive care.

The question came up again concerning Dan's accident. I didn't exactly tell Tim the true facts when he asked me about the funeral. I told him Dan's body had been flown back to his hometown. He expressed his sympathy, with a bashful grin. He walked me to my car. He requested with a hand on my shoulder, "now remember Maggie, if you need anything don't hesitate to call me." I nodded my head, "okay, I will, thank you."

I stopped by the supermarket on my way home. I needed so many things; I didn't know where to start. There were several people in the store, all starring at me. One of the ladies had two little girls with her and the one of girls approached me, saying..."my daddy said you are a witch." I dropped the dishwashing liquid on the floor. I was stun to hear such a thing. They think I am a witch, I thought. I understand why they gaped strangely as I enter the store. I didn't do anything. My grandfather casted a spell on them, I thought as I picked up the dishwashing liquid. They wouldn't believe me anyway. My dogs barked as I pulled up in the driveway. The radio was on. I was sure I had turned the radio off before I left this morning. I placed the groceries on the table. The map was still spreaded out on the table. Tomorrow will be a better day. Maybe, I will asked Tim to help me. I felt fatigued. A short nap might perk my energy up. I dreamed I was in a strange valley. A place I had never seen before. There were little children all around me. No adults, just little kids. I was standing in the center surrounded by the children. The strangest thing about the children, they had no eyes, but they could see me. They were running and jumping all over the place. While standing there I looked down and under my feet was a blanket. I touched the blanket...oh, I thought...this is my grandfather's old tattered blanket. The colors and designs appeared the same. Suddenly the children were silent. I glanced up and the children boasted with very happy expressions on their faces. One of the little girls pulled my hand and with a bashful grim she uttered, "mother, mother, you are here. We have been waiting for you." All of the children bowed down on their knees and shouted, "mother we love you." "No, no, I shouted. I am not your mother. No, no." I woke up from my dream. Sweat was pouring down my face. I sat up quickly, "oh my God, what is the meaning of this dream?" Maybe, it's a sign that I will become a mother in the future.

I poured myself a glass of water. So much as happened to me. First, I was called a witch and in my dream I was a mother. What does it mean? My mind was confused. Suddenly someone knocked on the door. "Who is it, I asked?" I recognized the voice as Tim Carter's. He had helped Dan on the farm. He replied, "hi Maggie, I stopped by to see how you are doing. Do you need a helping hand?" "Tim glanced around the farm. "Look like you need some serious repairs on that fence." "Oh yes Tim, things are in need of a repairman. Come on in. Would you like some breakfast?" Tim uttered in a neighborly tone, "well, I ate early this morning, but the long walk has built an enormous appetite." "That's wonderful, I beamed. There is plenty leftover on the stove. I am happy you stopped by. I need someone to talk to." Tim followed me into the kitchen. I fixed a large plate of leftovers. I continued, "Tim, I have been under a lot of stress since Dan's death. Life is so lonely without my grandparents." Tim gazed at me with a sad look in his eyes. He replied, "I know it must be hard on your nervous living out here all by yourself. Why don't you think about selling the farm?" I nervously rubbed my hands together. "Well, selling the farm is what got me into this problem right now." Tim nodded his head not sure of what I was talking about. I didn't want to get into that subject.

◆

CHAPTER 10
"A TOUCH OF POWER"

I quickly changed the conversation. "How is your mother?" Tim swallowed the last piece of bacon. He responded, "we brought her home yesterday. She is still very weak. The stroke left her paralyzed on her right side. We tried to take care of her, but you know how Mama is. She wants things done her way or not at all." I poured myself a cup of coffee. Tim glanced up from his coffee cup. "Maggie, there is something else that you are not telling me, isn't it?" I responded, "yes Tim, you know my grandfather's death has never been solved. The policemen are convinced that it was an accident. His blanket and gun was never found. I believe my grandfather's spirit is wandering around this earth. His spirit will not rest until the woods give up the secret of the past. Tim retorted, "I don't believe in the dead coming back. Once you die you are done with on this earth. There's no more walking or talking on this earth, girl. Your grandfather is dead." "No, I exclaimed, I know there's a secret that he wants me to find in those woods, or somewhere on this land." Tim looked very surprised as I blabbered on about my feelings.

"I have proof...let me show you something that I found in my grandfather's old chest." I pulled the map out of the drawer. "Look at this spot that's marked off. Where do you think this location is?" Tim examined the map and scratched his head and boasted, "I think I know exactly where that spot is...Maggie you might have something here. It won't hurt to check it out. When do you want to start?" I respected Tim. He offered to help me, even though he didn't believe in the dead coming back. I quickly answered, "as soon as possible." Tim walked towards the door, "well, will tomorrow be too soon...around noon?" "That's fine with me," I answered.

I couldn't help thinking about the wired dream I had...children without eyes, yet they could see. That's impossible I thought. I took the clothes out of the washing machine and hung them on the line. The sun was very hot and it wouldn't take them long to dry. While outside I noticed the flowers had commenced to blooming on the trees. Now, I understand why my grandfather loved the outdoors. I walked around the farm as I remembered my grandparents. Being outside made me really miss them. The time passed by quickly.

Maybe I will go and visit Tim's mother today. I haven't talked with her since she had the stroke. Mrs. Carter has five boys and no girls. Therefore, she took care of all the housework and the cooking herself. I know she could use my help. I baked two pies and a cake for her. Tim was working outside. He noticed me and said, "good evening, Maggie its good to see you again so soon. Do we still have a trip to the woods tomorrow?" I answered, "why yes, I will see you then." I knocked on the door and the youngest son answered. "Hi, Mrs. Maggie, Mama is in the living room." Mrs. Carter yelled, "who is it, Mike?" "Its Mrs. Forest, and she brought you a cake and some pies." He invited me in and at the same time he was trying to take the cake and pies out of my hands. "No Mike, let give it to your mother." Mrs. Carter was sitting in a chair. She was very excited to see me. She wonders why I hadn't been over to see her sooner. Mrs. Carter had loss a lot of weight and her body appeared thin and weak. However, she still had a big smile. I gave her a big hug and she began to cry within seconds and I was crying too. The stroke had left her paralyzed on her left side.

I wished there were something I could do for her. She was my dearest friend. I sat down besides her with tears running down my face. I asked, "Mrs. Carter is there anything I can do?" She answered, "Maggie, I have been very sick. I just thank God for the strength to be here right now. The stroke left me where I can't get around. I haven't been to church for awhile." She looked at her limp arm. I reached out and wiped away her tears. I touched her limp arm and massaged it gently. Suddenly, Mrs. Carter fell back in her chair as if someone had knocked her down. I shouted, "what's wrong, Mrs. Carter?" Her eyes rolled back in her head and finally she took a deep breath. "Lord Jesus, thank you,

Maggie your hands were so hot. I felt something in my arm all the way down to my toes. I felt the sensation myself. I requested, "close your eyes and relax." I sensed her emotions. She closed her eyes and rested her head back on the chair. I gripped her hand again and as I message her hand I felt the heat from my hands. She slowly moved her fingers and her arm. She opened her eyes and screamed, "oh my God, I can move my arm. She raised her hands in the air. Suddenly, Mrs. Carter jumped up from her chair and shouted, "look, I can walk, I can walk." All the children hurried inside. Tim appeared confused. He cried, "Mama, you are walking. How did this happen?" He ran to his mother and hugged her. All the other brothers were delighted. Mike yelled, "this is a miracle."

Mrs. Carter smiled, "Maggie, how did you do that?" I blabbered, "oh nothing, I just massaged the weak muscles in your arm that was caused by the stroke." Mrs. Carter sat down to catch her breath. After all the jumping around, she uttered, "no, no, Maggie, it was more. My doctor has been massaging my arms for two months and nothing happen. I felt the heat from your hands go through my body. "Girl, you got some type of power." "Thank you Jesus for sending her to me."

While sitting on the sofa, Nick asked, "how did you do that? Are you a doctor?" I replied, "oh no, anyone can massage the muscles. Let me show you. I reached out for his hand, and he pulled away. "Don' t be afraid of things you don't understand, I uttered with a smile. Mrs. Carter prayed from one room to another. She thanked God for her recovery.

Shortly afterwards, I left the Carter's farm and drove home. I could not believe what had happen. The signs of power have been given to me. I acted as if someone else had taken over my body. The spirit of my grandfather was there with me. I looked at my hands and thought, if I had power to heal Mrs. Carter, maybe I can heal the men at the hospital. The spirit of my grandfather has ascended upon me. The power of the blanket is concealed in my hands. I am the blanket. My grandfather's words have been revealed. The mystery of the blanket lies in the spirit of my future generation. I remember when Dan tried to kill me. The spirit untied my hands. I experience the touch of heat on my hands. My dream symbolized the rebirth of my future.

After I arrived home, I went to my grandfather's room I pulled the box from under the bed. I looked closely at the arrowhead. It showed a child's face, a face without eyes. "What does this mean," I thought? I held the arrowhead in my hand and my hands began to feel warm. At that very moment I thought about the men in the hospital. I really wanted to help them. My mind was set, so I drove to the hospital as fast as I could. The nurse noticed me coming down the hall. She glanced up, "oh, you stop by to visit again." "That's so wonderful of you to think about them. No one seems to know what is wrong." I smiled as I walked down the hall. I slowly opened the door. The youngest policeman lay there with his eyes closed. I touched him lightly on his forehead. He stared at me. I uttered, "don't be afraid." "I won't hurt you." He closed his eyes and quickly opened them again. I pressed both hands against his forehead. I felt the power working. He quickly sat up in the bed and asked, "now, what can I do for you today, miss?" He glanced around the room. "Hey, um...I am in a hospital...why am I here?" "I am not sick." I didn't have time to explain. I rushed out the door. He ringed for the nurse. The nurse ran to his room.

Through all the excitement no one paid me any attention. I slipped into the other policeman's room. He stared at the ceiling with no expression on his face. I walked closer to his bed and placed my hand on his forehead. He didn't move, but suddenly yelled out, "what in the hell is going on here?" "Who are you?" "I am here to help you, sir...you are in a hospital." He pulled the sheet back, "I want out of this bed," he demanded. I ran out of his room. He followed me down the hall trying to put on his robe. The nurse guided him back to his room. He remembered his name and everything about himself.

The nurses were puzzled. They didn't know how to explain these recoveries. Time was running out. I had to move quickly because my plan was to heal the other man. I hurried to his room. He looked like a pale ghost as I approached his bed. Without a word, I placed my hand on his forehead. He struggled around in the bed. I felt the sensation exploring through my body. Now, my job was completed. On my way out the door, I glanced back and he was scrambling around for his glasses. I avoided the nurses by using the stairway out of the hospital. No one noticed me. My heart beat rapidly as I ran to my car. I speeded down the highway smiling at myself in the mirror. "I did it...I healed them." I continued to stare at my hands. They appeared the same.

On my way home, I thought about the map. I had plans to go to the woods with Tim. When I arrived, Tim was sitting on the steps. "I almost left," he said. "I have been waiting for you to come home for at least two hours." "I'm sorry, Tim." "I lost track of the time. You know how time pass when you're shopping." I said, "give me a minutes to change into my jeans." Tim took the shovel from the barn and said, "let me see the map again to make sure we are going in the right direction." As he studied the map, Tim rubbed his forehead. "Maggie, that's a long walk...maybe we should drive the truck to the edge of the woods." That sounds fine to me because I was already tired from the running around at the hospital. I replied, "you can drive the truck."

♦

CHAPTER 11
"THE CONSPICIOUS LIGHT"

Tim drove through the bumpy road to the woods. I sat quietly thinking about what had happened at the hospital. He parked the truck on the edge of the road and as we entered the woods, I walked slowly behind him. He then whispered, "did you hear that sound?" I replied, "no, what sound. I didn't hear anything." Tim stumbled over a tree branch. He whispered, "it sounds like voices." We continued to walk not sure of where we were. The leaves cracked under our feet as we ambled across the dead branches.

The smell of wild berry filled the air. I walked behind Tim and I noticed a bright light under on of the big trees. I grabbed him by the shoulder and said, "Tim, did you see that light?" He peeped between the branches and responded in a nervous tone...."no, there's no light, not that I can see." I dashed ahead of him. "Come on Tim, dig here in this spot." He asked, "why this spot?" He couldn't see the light. I believed the light was a sign to dig under this tree. He didn't ask me anymore questions, even though he was fearful and ready to leave the woods as soon as possible. I watched him as he tossed the soil. The ground was very soft because of the rain last week.

The light disappeared as the hold became larger. Tim dug deeper into the ground. I asked, "can you feel anything with the shovel?" He raked the shovel across the bottom of the hole. Suddenly, he shouted, "hey, wait a minute...I think I feel something." I sat down on the ground near him. I touched his shoulder. Tim jumped back from me with his eyes wide opened with fear. "Maggie, your...hands. Ugh...they are very hot." I pretended not to hear him. I yelled, "Tim, come out of the hole." He had a puzzled look on his face, as he rolled out of the hole. I spread my hands over the hole. The box ascended from the bottom of the hole. Tim's hands began to tremble. His mouth bolted open in shock. Finally, he uttered, "ugh...ugh...Mag...how did you do that?" The box floated above the hole. He drooped down on the ground shaking with his eyes fasten on the box. I called out, "Tim, don't be afraid. I can explain what you are witnessing. I have the gift from my grandfather's spirit." He goggled at me as if I was someone else. "What spirit," he retorted." "Oh, Tim it's a long story, I responded." "Come and help me opened the box." As he reached out to help me, a bright light appeared knocking him down on the ground. He couched down on his knees and covered his head. "Come on Tim, help me," I screamed. He advanced towards the box again and the light swiped him across the face. He groaned, "what was that, someone slapped me." I was frightened for him. I shouted, "stay away Tim, don't come near the box." I wasn't afraid for myself. After all I have seen a lot of strange things happen since my grandfather's death.

I opened the box and it was filled with money, thousands of dollars. Tim peeped over my shoulder and he whispered, "what's in the box?" I grabbed a handful of money and threw it into the air. "Lots of money," I sizzled. Tim slowly picked up a handful of money. "Maggie, whose money is this?" "I don't know, I snapped quickly." "My grandfather intended for me to find this box." "Maybe, it belonged to him." As I pulled the money from the box, I noticed a note at the bottom that read, "whoever finds this box is blessed with the spirit of Sanato." Tim beamed frantically, "what does Sanato means?" He stared at me with a bemused look in his eyes and blabbered, "Maggie, you have some type of power, don't you?" "Are you...ugh...ugh...a witch?" I answered him quickly, "no, I am not a witch. I can't explain it. Let's go back in the house."

Tim lurched slowly behind me carrying the box. Every step I enacted, I wondered what was he thinking. I broke the silence. "Tim, one day you will understand what happened here today. Please don't tell anyone about what happened. Keep this a secret between us, okay?" He nodded his head.

◆

CHAPTER 12

"THE GIFT"

We returned to the truck and Tim was very quiet. I asked, "Tim, would you like to own this truck?" He pointed, "you mean this truck? Yeah, one day I am going to buy me one just like this baby." I opened the box again and in a meek voice said, "Tim, you see all this money. I can buy anything I want. I have thousands of dollars right here in this box." Tim surprisingly asked, "your grandfather had something to do with this. I know I'm right. Is this the mysterious affect from your grandfather's blanket? Does the blanket have something to do with your powers?" I rubbed my hands together, "Tim, I am going to help people, not harm them."

My grandfather's spirit is at rest now. The woods have given up its secret. The sun was almost down when we returned home. Tim carried the box inside. As he prepared to leave, he stunned me with a kiss on my cheek. "I hope you will be okay," he uttered. I smiled, "sure, I will be fine." I pulled the keys from my pocket and passed them to Tim. "You don't have to walk home...here take my truck." He looked at me very strangely and said, "Maggie, I don't mind walking home." I beamed, "Tim, the truck is yours. I am giving it to you as a gift." He pulled at his ears. "Did I hear you right?" He asked again, "did you say you are giving me your truck?" "Yes, I replied, it's yours if you want it.

Remember to keep my secret about what happen here today."
Tim embraced me, "Maggie, your secret will always remain a
secret in my heart forever. I will see you tomorrow...I have a
couple more fences to repair, he responded.

As I walk towards the steps, I glanced back to see Tim
driving away. The night was very beautiful. I remained
outside for awhile looking over the yard. I was shocked at the
amount of money that we found buried in the woods. I
couldn't help but wonder whom did the money belong to. I
read the note again. What does Sanato mean? The thought
was heavy on my mind. I went into my grandfather's room.
Maybe I overlooked something. I checked the closet and
drawers again. As I reached down to pull out another drawer,
I felt something taped to the top of the drawer. I pulled out
the drawer and a small book was attached to the inside. I
rapidly opened the book. The name Sanato was written on
the front page. A drawing of a face without eyes appeared on
the next page. My dream I thought. The children without
eyes in my dream...what does it mean? Was this part of my
future?"

The book revealed things I didn't understand. I put
the book away in a safety place. It's been a long day for me. I
dashed into the living room just in time to tune in on the
news. I wanted to know if the men had been dismissed from
the hospital. The spokesperson stated that the men had
recovered very mysteriously. No one at the hospital could
explain what happen. The nurse stated, "they regained their
memories after a visit from a young lady in her mid twenties,
weighting about 125 lbs., and about 5'3" tall with medium

length black hair." The nurse continued, "whatever she did made them well, I am sure of that."

The men rejoined their families. They didn't remember me or what had happen to them. I prepared myself a sandwich and poured a glass of milk. As I sat down the box of money registered in my mind. I counted the money over again, after six times and never coming up with the same amount. I decided to stop.

I wandered around the room looking at the ceiling and the worn out wallpaper. My grandmother and I hung the paper many years ago. I thought, I am going to sell this farm and move away from all the bad memories of Dan. I stuffed the money inside a large bag...thinking to myself, it will be safe here. The first thing tomorrow I will go to the bank and deposit it in my account. I didn't realize the time had slipped by so quickly. I made sure the doors were locked and retired to bed.

The next morning Tim repaired the fence. I watched him as he worked. He pulled off his shirt and I had never noticed his body until today. His masculine physique caught my eyes. I didn't have the power to turn away. I watched him as he wiped the sweat from his forehead. Tim was eight years older than I was, but he looked very young for his age. He had a babylike face nested under curly hair. I realized my lifestyle was at its lowest stage. I am still young and there is no reason for me to barricade myself. My intimate thoughts weaken my fleshy body, devising a mood. I was not able to deviate the deep images from my mind. I thought, maybe Tim would enjoy having dinner with me. A desperate plot, I thought. I slipped into my sundress and piled my hair on top of my head...the style always made me appear taller and sexy. I dabbed a little of Grandma's perfume behind my ears. I admired myself in the mirror and was very please with the way I looked. My breasts filled out my dress in all the right spots. My mind flashed back, Dan you foolish man. You had it all and lost it because you became too greedy.

My grandmother always said, the way to a man heart is through his stomach. I will cook Tim a wonderful dinner. Maybe, he will notice how pretty I am today. After all, I am a young woman and beautiful, too. I looked through the refrigerator and there was nothing to cook...well, nothing that would impress Tim. I made a list of some of the things I needed to pick up at the grocery store. I will bake a chicken. I rushed off to the store leaving the door unlock just in case Tim wanted some water. When I arrived the store was very crowded. I picked up a bottle of champagne. I gazed around me and noticed a man standing in line who looked like the man who drove the ambulance that night. I asked, "sir, how are you?" He smiled and replied, "fine and how are you?" He didn't recognize me from the hospital. I quickly turned my head. He just doesn't remember how sick he really was. He was strapped down in his bed. I moved back in line behind the little short lady. She starred at me and said, "hi, my name is Lisa Green." I smiled and said, "my name is Maggie Johnson. I am very happy to meet you." I noticed the cane in one hand and that her leg had a deformity which made walking difficult without the use of the cane. Finally she asked, "are you the young lady everyone is calling a witch?"

"She grinned and showed her tobacco stain teeth. "You don't look like an evil person. As a matter of fact, you seem like a real nice lady to me." I rubbed my hands nervously together and casted my eyes around the store. Most of the people were leaving. Suddenly, a thought popped in my head...show her you are not an evil person. Now is the time, but how am I going to achieve this without drawing a lot of attention?" I noticed she had a bag of oranges in her hand. I will guide her from the crowd, I thought. Directed by my conceived mind, I touched her on the shoulder. "Miss, one of the oranges is rotten in your bag. I can help you pick out a better bag of oranges." I gazed down at the oranges and she uttered, "okay, I didn't know the oranges were rotten."

Lisa Green's wooden cane produced a loud sound as she followed me to the back. I gathered up several bags of oranges and she inspected each bag slowly. I dropped my keys down by her feet. As I reached down to pick up my keys, I touched her deformity leg. I gripped her leg with both hands. A strange expression abruptly appeared on her face and she shouted, "what are you doing?" I glanced up, "please, please, keep your voice down." She dropped her cane on the floor. "Oh God, my leg ...it feels so...I... ugh...I don't know...it is hot. I can feel something happening to me. What...what are you doing to me?" She reached for her cane. I whispered, "you don't need your cane anymore. Look at your leg." She glanced down at her leg and pulled up her dress. The lady grabbed my hand an cried, "thank you Jesus for this lady...she's a saint." She picked up her cane and passed it to me. "Here, you keep this, I don't need it anymore."

I was pleased we didn't attract a lot of attention. A couple of people clustered around her asking questions. I quickly left her in the back of the store. I rushed to the cashier line to pay for my groceries. Before I could leave the store, Mrs. Green was back in line behind me. The cashier asked, "Mrs. Green, how are you today? I see you are walking without your cane." She answered, "I don't need a cane anymore." She pulled up her dress, "look, my leg is straight. Thanks to this lady right here," she blabbered. Pointing at her leg, the cashier responded, "how did you do that?" I boasted, "well, they call me a witch...maybe, I am a good witch." The cashier beamed, "wow! That's unreal."

With a surprised expression on my face, Mrs. Green followed me out of the store. "Honey, you are no witch," she assured me." "But, I would like to know your secret. You know about my leg." I replied, "Mrs. Green, it wasn't anything that I done. Just your faith in yourself." She stammered, "I'm not going to ask anymore questions. Ugh...all I know is I was cripple when I stepped in the store. But, I am walking out a whole woman, again." We promised each other we would stay in touch. With a bemused look on her face, she uttered, "I will see you again."

I couldn't explain the phenomenon of my touch. On the way home, I wandered about the stranger I met in the store. News spread very quickly. People will ask questions and want answers about what happened at the store today. I washed my hands and began preparing dinner. The phone ring and someone on the other end replied, "hello Mr. Forest, this is the news reporter from KKRV TV station. We would like to come by and talk with you. It would only take a few minutes of your time." I thought about it for a second, "yes, tomorrow will be fine," I replied.

Knowing what the people wanted to hear, I rushed outside to discuss the idea with Tim. He glanced up from his work, "what's wrong Maggie?" I shouted, "guess what...the reporter from the news station wants to come over and interview me." Tim responded, "now Maggie, what are they going to interview you about?" I paused for a second..."well, I touched this old lady's leg. I met her in the store today. One leg of hers was very crooked. I think I had a lot to do with her not needing a cane anymore. I just wanted to prove to her and the other people there, that I wasn't a witch. That's what they are calling me around town." Tim nodded his head. I smiled, "well, why not use the gift to do something good for somebody?" Tim starred at me with a strange look in his eyes; "you healed my mother. I knew something was not normal about her recovery. I just couldn't put my finger on it at that time." I nodded my head, "yes, but I didn't know at that time that I had the gift to heal. I was just as shocked as your mother was." He picked up the hammer without another word and he began tapping the nail in the pole. "I will call you when dinner is ready." Tim winked his eye, "okay."

I flounced back into the house. I hoped he noticed the clever and the curve my sundress exposed. The table was set with Grandma's finest china. Grandpa gave it to her for her 40th birthday. I called Tim in for dinner. He had an enormous appetite for such a small man. I piled his plate several times with potatoes and greens. When he finally finished, he smiled, "Maggie, that dinner was fantastic." He wiped his mouth with a napkin and said, "where did you learn to cook so wonderful?" I gracefully strolled from the table with the dishes, "oh, from my grandmother, of course." Tim eyes widen with pleasure. I had prepared his favorite dessert...banana pudding. It was just the way he liked it, with lots of cookies.

After dinner we talked about the reporter, and as the conversation progressed Tim asked me questions about the money. Because of the experience I had with Dan, I didn't go into direct details about the money. I asked him if he would go with me whenever I decided to go shopping for a new car. I discussed the thought of selling the farm one day. He asked, "where would you move?" "Maybe, to the windy city of Chicago," I answered. My uncle lived in Chicago. He would tell us how much he enjoyed the city life. How wild the people were on Saturday night. Tim listened quietly as I talked about moving. Suddenly he replied, "Maggie, I will miss you. We have become good friends in a special way. I smiled, "don't worry Tim, that's a long ways off." I have to find a buyer for the farm first, and I have no idea where to begin." He responded, "why don't you use the same real estate dealer...you know the one Dan tried to contact behind your back. Maybe they will still be interested in buying the farm." Tim asked, "do you still have the letter?" I smiled slightly at Tim...I must have told him earlier about the letter. I promised him that I would check the boxes of letters later.

♦

CHAPTER 13

"THE ROMANCE"

The day was almost gone. Tim and I had talked for a couple of hours. The time passed so quickly when you are having a good time. I strolled over to the ice bucket and took out a bottle of champagne. Tim beamed with a certain twinkle in his eyes. "Oh girl, you went all out on this dinner. Thank you so much for inviting me." I gave the bottle to him, and he opened it carefully. First, he poured me a glass...then himself. I sat down on the sofa and motion for Tim to follow me. I sipped my champagne slowly. It was just right, chilled just the way I liked it. I finished one glass and he poured me another one. He stared at me as he filled my glass again. I began to feel the effect of the alcohol. I quickly turned on the television. Tim requested to turn on the stereo instead. The soft music relaxed my tense muscles. Tim reached out his hand and whispered, "how about a dance beautiful lady?" "Oh yes, I boasted, this beats watching television anytime."

Tim and I danced to my favorite songs. He pulled me tighter as we danced...a lot closer than I expected him too. But, with the champagne I was totally relaxed. I pressed my head against his chest. The music and the champagne placed me in another world. He lifted up my face and kissed me on the cheek. The warmth from his body began to penetrate through my clothes. He wants me. The thought was both starling and novel that Tim Carter should find me desirable.

Oh course, he had never kissed me. But I have imagined what a thrill it must be...I recognized the way he looked at me. His hands tightened around my waist and I had no desire to push him away. I shifted a little closer, my hips brushing against the inside of his knee. Tim's reaction was almost indefinitely. But, I felt him shift...trying to maintain his balance. I felt the acute flare of sensitiveness in his touch. His eyes plunged to my mouth. It was one thing to acknowledge that he wanted me, but it was something else to know what to do with that desire. The truth is I wasn't particularly good at sex. But, at least Tim and I would experience the procedure together. Boosting up my nerves, I leaned forward and set my lips on his. For an instant, surprise kept him frozen. Feeling his stillness and mistaking the cause...Tim pressed his mouth firmer to minds as if he could force me to respond. His fingers were suddenly entangling in my hair, pulling my head back so that my mouth thrust upward. Struggling with my feelings, I lifted my lashes...dazzled by the excitement. I was afraid of what I might see in his eyes. I slowly opened my eyes. There was a display of embarrassed admiration in his eyes. But, there was something else there, too...a craving desire for something warm and soft, something like me. At that moment Tim whispered, "Maggie, you are so sexy and soft. I could spend the rest of my life nesting right here with you." I tried to hold on to my better judgement, I murmured, "so could I."

The process to discover more about me proceeded where Tim left off. He kissed me again, his mouth touch my lips lightly. Once, twice, and then again. He landed quick butterfly kisses that offered a tantalizing hint of cloud nine trips. Tim kissed first, one corner of my mouth and then the other. His lips trembled in anticipation of more to come. His fingers tugged gently at my hair, tilting my head back so that he could feather a line of light kisses along the edge of my throat. First, one side then the other. I had read books in which the author said that someone's bones were melting, but I never experienced the phenomenon myself until this moment. My finger curled into the fabric of his shirt as his teeth tugged gently at my ear. His breath escaped with the smell of champagne on his tongue...a tongue that teased me to the brink of a whimper. Tim continued his leisurely exploitation...brushing kisses along the arch of each brow. The curve of my cheek was building up tension within me until by the time he made his way back to my mouth I almost explored with relief. His teeth softly bit down on my lower lip...nibbling and tasting as if it were an exotic delicacy for him to savor. Dan never made me feel this way. I never felt anything like this. My nails dug deeply into Tim's shoulders sharply in unconscious demand. He continued to passionately kiss my lips. I arched my chin allowing Tim possession of me...demanding more.

Tim stopped for just a second, "are you trying to seduce me," he asked? Half out of my mind with desire, I whispered, "I don't know." "Well, you are," Tim softly spoke with uneasy breath. I let my hand slide from his shoulder to his chest. My fingers began working on the buttons of his shirt. I thought about what I was doing and was shocked by my own actions. I wasn't the kind of woman who would so such things as this. Well, um...um, it's a wonderful feeling. When I was married to Dan, he complained bitterly that I wasn't passive enough in bed and that I never initiated anything. Suddenly, it hit me. I never really wanted too, the way I wanted Tim. My hand touched Tim's chest and slowly rubbed over his heart. It thudded against my hand...reminding me of a tango dance. I whispered, "do you mind being seduced?" Tim cupped my face, "Baby, are you sure this is what you want?" I know he was asking about much more than this moment. He was asking if I was sure about the future...if I wanted to be married to him. I replied without any hesitation, "I'm sure this is what I want."

We both knew that we shouldn't jump into things too quickly. We should take things slow and easy. But, I hungered for the feeling of his arms around me. Tim's hand slid down my back...urging me closer until I was pressed against him with my thighs braced on either side of him. My eyes widen as I felt the rock-hard length of his erection pressed against me through the layers of clothing. I wanted to pull away...frightened by his genetic arousal. I was still for a moment as if the feel of him numbed me. "Wow," was all I could whispered. Tim scooped me into his arm and carried me to my bedroom holding me as if I weighted next to nothing. He quickly snapped off the light, laying me gently on the bed and undressing me careful as if this was my first time. It really was the first time in a sense. Certainly it was the first time I felt what I am feeling now. As Tim removed the last of my clothes, he murmured, "you are so beautiful," while he was trailing downward from my mouth to my breast.

Again, he whispered, "so lovely, touching my nipple with his tongue as sensation jolted through my body. My whole body tremble with pleasure. My breathing was coming in shallow puffs. I pleaded, "Tim...oh no...oh Tim." He murmured, "Ssshh"...and eased down on the bed while reaching for his belt and tearing at it with impatient fingers. Within seconds, Tim clothes were lying in a pile on the floor. He was all over me, easing my legs apart with his knees. I felt his arousal press against me. I thought with a smile on my face, "rock, oh no, hard rock." Tim, without another small second of waiting, sheathed himself in my body with one long gliding trust...filling me completely. My eyes widened as I stared at Tim. I was stunned by the powerful sensation. Tim whispered..."okay, okay?" I managed to say..."y...ye...yes." He didn't need any other response. Bracing his weight on his elbows, Tim began to move within me. I gave myself to him without reservation, no shit, no pretending...just simply Maggie...so innocence...truly a widow in passion. I began to reach my highest point and Tim groaned with pleasure. We laid without speaking listening to the ragged sound of each other breathing. Finally, Tim found the strength to sit up. He replied, "Girl, you are remarkably wonderful. If you get any better at this, I will need a wheelchair before I'm forty." I tossed my hair from my face, "I guess this mean we are more than just friends." Tim responded, "you are my everything." He was waiting for me to test him with more questions, but instead I merely lay there and thought with a flash...Tim might not be in love with me. But I care for him and given enough time and the right nurturing, I could grow to love him." We laid in each other arms. Tim gently stroked my hair. He whispered, "girl, it was wonderful." I was speechless with a million thought whirling through my head.

Lovemaking never felt so real. I wanted it to happen over and over again. The sound of rain caught my attention. I didn't realize it was pass 2:00 a.m. Tim asked, "would you like for me to leave?" I reacted, "I hope you never leave me." Tim pressed me firmly against his body. He responded, "baby, as long as you want me. I will be here for you." He had voiced the words I wanted to hear. Now it was up to me to believe him. I wanted to trust him more than anything in this world. I made up my mind that night...Tim will stay with me tonight and all the other nights to come. We slept in each other arms.

The sunrise awakens me, but I didn't want that moment to end. Tim opened his eyes, "good morning, beautiful lady...you were wonderful last night." I closed my eyes and snuggled closer to him. He murmured, "baby, I hope it wasn't the champagne. The things you said last night, did you mean them? "How do you feel about me now?" I answered, "I feel the same. What about you?" Tim sits up, "come here, girl. I would have married you last night if you had asked me too. My heart is feeling the love I have for you. I know it is real, baby. Maggie Forest, I love you very much. It didn't just happened last night." Tim kissed me on my breast and my whole body quivers with pleasure. We made love again.

In my mind, there was nothing else I wanted more except maybe a hot shower. I walked sluggishly towards the bathroom. I began to feel sick in my stomach. I eyed myself in the mirror. "What's wrong with me," I thought? I wondered if it was something that I ate last night or maybe the champagne. I pulled my robe up slowly and wandered into the kitchen for a cup of coffee. The hot coffee will perk me up, I thought. As I sipped the coffee, I began to feel even worse.

I heard Tim taking a shower. I sat down at the table...what's wrong with me? My body felt drain of all my energy. Tim stepped through the doorway with a big grin on his face. "Good morning beautiful lady, how are you feeling?" He gave me a big hug. "Okay, what the lonesome face for?" He kissed me lightly on my forehead. Tim expression abruptly changed. He uttered, "hey Maggie, is something wrong? You don't look so good." I blabbered, "everything is fine. Oh, I was just thinking about our relationship. I hope we both feel the same about each other." Tim sat down besides me and reached for my hand. He replied, "baby, when I worked with your husband, I always noticed how beautiful you were. I never dreamed that you would be a part of my life. I am a lucky man and I owe it all to you. Please, say you will be mind forever," he pleaded. I braced back the tears and between kisses, I murmured, "Tim, I never thought you noticed me. I am happy you are here. Let's try to make the best of our life together." Tim walked around the table. "Oh, I saw you alright. I admired you more than you will ever know. At that time you were a married woman." I reacted, "well, I am not married now." Tim eyes lit up and he said, "how would you like to get married?" I responded, "Tim, are you joking? Get married?" He replied, "why not, baby." I sprung from my seat giving him a big hug. "Yes, I will marry you," I boasted. Tim picked me up from the floor and whirled me around. He spluttered nervously, "yes...ugh...yes, let's do it girl," he uttered frantically.

"Maggie, Maggie, what's wrong?" I murmured, "I'm experiencing sharp pains in my stomach." Tim responded, "maybe it was something you ate last night or the champagne." I rubbed my stomach, "no, it's different from any other pain I have ever experienced." I clenched my teeth together...as I was frozen from the piercing pain in my stomach. Tim held my hand, while gazing me in the eyes. "Maggie, we didn't use any protection last night. Girl, you might have conceived a child." "Stop joking," I demanded. "I wouldn't feel like this the very next day. It's got to be something else." Tim glanced at me as I proceeded towards the bathroom. "Maggie, if you are serious about this, why not have a doctor check you?"

As time passed the pain subsided. I began to feel like my old self again. Tim vowed, "I'm going to stay with you anyway...even though you are feeling better." I embraced Tim, "yes, please stay with me. You don't ever have to leave." Tim answered, "well, I don't have any changing clothes." "Don't worry about clothes, I assured Tim. I will buy you all new clothes." Tim eyes lit up like a small child surprised by his first bicycle. He touched my hands while staring at me with those big brown eyes. He stammered, "Girl...ugh...how...ugh, how can I be so lucky." I smiled, "well you know the old saying, good things come to those who wait, or good things come in small packages...meaning little old me." Tim kissed me again...and again we ended up back in the bedroom and the time slipped away.

That was the beginning of a new romance for me. We enjoyed every moment of our time together. We lived in our own little world for three weeks. This was three weeks of unbelievable romantic moments. Finally, we decided to surface from our love nest. We visited Tim's mother first, to let her know that he was still alive. She looked up as we walked into the room. She embraced me and said, "Maggie, it's good to see you again. Then she shouted at Tim, "where have you been...at least you could have called." Tim looked perplexed, "well, I've been around...I'm sorry, Mama. I should have called you earlier. I told Mike to tell you that I was okay." Mrs. Carter demanded, "yes, he told me, but you should have been concerned about your family." Tim replied, "now Mom don't be angry with me. I am fine. Now let me tell you the good news. Maggie and I are getting married." Mrs. Carter sat down quickly. "Getting married, are you all sure about this. Marriage is a serious step." Tim responded, "yes Mama, we thought about it a lots. I love her very much. I want to spend the rest of my life with her." Mr. Carter folder her arms and looked directly at me. She asked, "Maggie, are you happy with my boy? Now, I am here to tell you that sometimes he can be very stubborn. Just like his father." I hugged Mrs. Carter, I'm sure we will get alone just fine," I smiled. We really try hard to communicate with each other. That's the key to a good relationship." Mrs. Carter nodded her head...as to say she agreed with me. She asked, "when are you getting married?" Tim yelled across the room, "real soon!" I nodded my head, "yes, we don't want to wait any longer than we have to."

Tim's youngest brother, Mike came into the room. He lustfully glanced over my body, as if he could see through my dress. He beamed, "yes, my big brother has good taste in woman." He looked down at my legs with a erotic gleam in his eyes. Tim gave him a push and made his way over to me. He kissed me while giving Mike a diverse look. "Yes, this is going to be my wife." We chatted on and on about the wedding arrangement.

After visiting with Mrs. Carter we drove to town and picked up our marriage license. Tim was surprised when I asked him to stop by the jewelry store. I wanted to see the most expensive ring sets in the store. Tim didn't have any money so he thought. The night before, I had stuffed a large sum of money in his wallet. He wandered around behind me. After looking at several rings, I gapped, "this is the one for me." Tim stared at the price and scratched his head and whispered, "Maggie, I don't have any money. I can't buy this ring today." Are you sure, I asked?" Tim pulled out his wallet, "okay, take a look, Tim shouted." "Money...oh, Maggie you put this in my wallet, didn't you?" I laughed, "no, Tim, no I didn't touch your wallet." Tim responded, "you probably used your super power to zap it in." I grinned as the clerk gloated at us with a peculiar expression on his face. He eyed us as if we were thieves. Then he asked, "would you like to get that set?" I boasted, "yes, we will take both sets." The clerk uttered in an excited tone, "gee, you must really love

this woman. These are some of our most impalpable sets."
Tim responded, "oh yes Sir; I love her very much." I smacked
Tim on the rear end; "I love you, too." The store manager
watched us from another room while we kissed. I know we
surprised the store manager by paying cash for the rings.

◆

CHAPTER 14

"A WHISPER FROM WITHIN"

We behaved like two down to earth black people. We
were happy and were acting just like kids having a good time
in a candy store. Suddenly, I felt a sharp pain in the bottom
of my abdomen. I couldn't stand up. I dropped down to my
knees and Tim grabbed my arms. "Maggie, Maggie, what's
wrong?" My mouth felt dry and I whispered in a rigorously
tone. "Tim, I don't know...I ...my...stomach...the pain...ugh."
The manager and the clerk rushed over. "Mama is there
something we can do? Are you okay?" Tim helped me to a
chair. "Maggie, are you okay?" I yawned. The pain was like a
ball of fire burning through my stomach. Something is not
right, I thought. Tim insisted, "I'm taking you home, Girl.
We are going to have to make an appointment to see a doctor
tomorrow."

The clerk thanked us for our business and placed the
rings in a big. Tim was closed mouthed as we drove home. I

broke the silent, "okay, I will go to the doctor. Maybe I'm coming down with a stomach virus or something." Tim responded, "you need to have yourself examined by a doctor. This is not something we can overlook." When we arrived home, a white car was parked in our driveway. I quickly asked, "who is that?" Tim answered, "it looks like a woman in the car." We stopped the car. The lady got out of her car and approached us. I recognized the lady from the store. She smiled, "Mama, I don't remember your name, but you changed my life one day at the grocery store. Will you please try to help my granddaughter? I know you can help her. Please, you are a God sent angel."

This woman had so much faith in me I couldn't let her down. She held her granddaughter in her arms. " She was born this way. I know you have the gift to make her walk. Please try for her sake. She has never walked in her life. You healed my deformity leg." She pleased and pleased for my help. She pointed at the little girl legs...look at her legs. I love her so much. She is my life and I am going to do whatever I can to help her. "Can you help her."

I remembered her name. "Mrs. Green, please allow my husband to help you." She followed us inside and sits on the sofa. Tim placed the little girl besides her. I walked over to the little girl. I asked, "what is your name?" She looked up at me with her big brown eyes. She declared, "my name is Bonnie." I brushed her dark curly hair from her face. My god, this child was so beautiful, I thought. I massaged her little legs...they were very small and limp. I lifted up her feet and gently caress them. She showed no sign of fear. I rubbed her tiny legs but felt nothing. She sits there staring at me. The protected grandmother was so nervous that she asked, "is anything happening?" Tim glanced at me over the little girl's shoulder. He looked very concerned. I thought for a minute. Something is wrong, nothing is happening. I insisted, "Tim, please take Mrs. Green in the kitchen." I need to concentrated on what I am doing. I could feel my stomach tighten up. As I continued to massage the little girl legs she remained very quite. Her eyes pursued my face as she watched my expression. Something is still wrong, I thought. I sit besides the little girl. She gazed at me, "please help me to walk. I can't play with my friends. They all call me names because I can't walk." Tears began to roll down her cheeks and I wiped her face while trying to fight back my tears. The little girl requested, "you can make me walk, I know you can. You helped grandmother's leg. Her leg was curved-in. She couldn't walk without her cane and you helped her. Please, help me too." The stress was building up and my head began to ache. I held her hand and promised her that I would try another time. I called Tim and Mrs. Green back into the room. She asked with a disappointing tone, "what's wrong...nothing happen?" "I'm sorry Mrs. Green, I uttered. Things just didn't work out for her. Maybe we can try again soon." Mrs. Green expressed anxiously, "I will bring her back to you another day. Thank you for trying."

I went to bed early. The pains had started again. I held my stomach. Oh God, what is happening to me? My face began to flushed. Tim rushed into the bedroom. He touched my face, "my God, Maggie you are burning up. I am going to take you to see a doctor right now," he demanded. I didn't want to go to a doctor. I beg Tim not to take me, I just wanted to rest. As I laid there in the bed, I began to think. It's been almost six weeks since we made love. I checked the date on the calendar and my cycle was two weeks late. I remember the first time Tim and I made love. I felt the same type of pains. The next day Tim called the reporter and cancelled the interview. The pain was more intense which really was terrific for me. Tim cuddled me in his arms.

I dreamed about the little girl and in my dream she was running around, jumping up and down on the swing set in the front yard. She was shouting, "you did it. You made me walk. Look at my legs. The children don't call me names anymore. Thank you, thank you." She kissed me several times on the cheeks. I must have slept for several hours. When I woke up Tim was holding me in his arms. He glanced down and whispered, "how are you feeling? You had me scare there for a minute. Were you dreaming?" I wiped my eyes, "yes, I had an envision. The little girl was in my dream."

Tim caressed my stomach. "I am worried about you, Girl. I think you need to go see a doctor." Without a fuss, I responded, "yes, I think so. I will make an appointment tomorrow. I am two weeks late for my cycle. My energy level is low. It seems like something or someone have drained all my strength from my body." Tim directed his attention to me. His manner expressed a serious side. "Maggie, you don't need to keep putting this off any longer. I have always been stubborn when it came time to go to the doctor. My mother and father would force a beating upon me to get me to go with them. I remember when I was ten years old and my tonsils had to be removed. When the doctor checked my throat, I was fighting like a bull. The nurse had to hold me down in the chair. My parents took me home and promised they would never take me to the doctor again."

Suddenly, Tim touched me on the shoulder, "Maggie, are you listening to me? Baby, what are you daydreaming about?" He replied, "now, you said you are two weeks late. Girl, I wonder, you just might be pregnant." I answered, "well, we didn't use any protection that first time, remember?" I closed my eyes. Tim uttered, "yes, I remember. You might be right. We will let the doctor find out what's really happening inside you." I finally pulled myself up off the bed. Tim watched me as I walked to the kitchen. He murmured in a surly manner, "look like you have lost some weight, too." I nodded my head. I poured myself a glass of water. As I entered the doorway, Tim said, "Maggie why don't we go ahead and get married. We have our license...what are we waiting for?" Tim put his arms around me. "Okay lady, if you feel better we will get married tomorrow." We really didn't have anything to wait for. I believed Tim would make me a good husband. He is so concerned about me. We have become very close in the short time that we have been together. He looked at me with those big brown eyes and said, "marry me Maggie. I will make you the happiest woman on earth. Darling, I will be the happiest man in the world. You want ever have to worry abut anything." He kissed me on my cheek. I believe you love me, too. He put his arms around me and kissed me again. He continued, "Maggie, you don't have to worry. I am nothing like Dan. I know the memories of your marriage to Dan are still fresh in your mind. I understand you might have doubts about me. First, I am grateful for all you've done. I don't know what my life would be like right now if you hadn't been a part of it."

I began to cry. Tim wiped the tears away. "Maggie, don't cry, please. I care for you, Baby. I will always stand by your side." Tim held me close and gently massaged my stomach. I thought about my grandparents and that I missed them so much. I guess Grandpa's spirit is at rest. I have not heard or seen any signs of him. I know he is watching over me. Some nights when the house is still, I can feel his presence. He makes sure I am okay. He promised me before he died that he would be with me always.

The next morning we ate a quick breakfast. I was eager to see the doctor. We were the first to arrive. The nurse was a short plump woman with a very thin hairline. Her glasses dangled low on the bridge of her nose. She looked up from her papers and said, "hi, may I help you?" Tim replied, "we are here to see Dr. Biblog." She answered in a masculine voice, "will you please sign in on this chart, I will be with you shortly." I filled out the forms and within a few seconds she asked me to follow her. Tim stayed in the waiting room while I followed her down the hall. She signaled me into one of the waiting room that was very small. There really wasn't room enough for two people. I sat down in the chair beside the little desk. The nurse asked, "what type of problem are you having?" I uttered, "it's my abdomen...sometimes I have severe pain." The nurse requested, "where are you having these pains?" I distinguish the lower part of my abdomen. The nurse asked, "when do you experience pain?" I replied, "most of the time after I have sex." The nurse wrote down everything on the chart. She asked, "how long have you been feeling these pains?" "I guess about three or four weeks," I responded. The nurse took my blood pressure and urine sample. She told me to wait in the waiting room. The doctor would be with me in a few minutes. Before she left, she gave me a gown to put on. I undressed and put the paper gown on. The room began to feel cold and I pulled the sheet up around my legs. After watching the ceiling for what I thought was forever, the nurse open the door and the doctor walked in behind her. He was a tall thin man with his head ball on the top. He replied in a deep voice, "Mrs. Forest, I am Dr. Bigliog. "So you are having pains in your abdomen. I want you to relax and lay back," he ordered. I thought to myself, relax Maggie...there is no way you can relax. When someone is poking his finger in you private parts. I closed my eyes through the examination. Finally he uttered, "Mrs. Forest you can sit up now. I want you to get dressed and I will be right back to talk with you."

This time the waiting was even longer. My patience began to fade. As I waited for the results of the test, my palms began to sweat. Finally I heard footsteps approaching the door and I nervously bounced in the chair. The doctor closed the door behind him. I thought to myself, "oh Lord, here it comes." I goggled up at the doctor. With a slight frown on his face the doctor replied in a lighthearted tone, "Mrs. Forest, you are going to have a baby." The reason you are tired all the time is that your blood iron is low." He continued, "I'm going to write you a prescription. This will help to increase your iron level."

The thought hit me like a hammer on my head...I am pregnant. I am going to have a baby. The nurse smiled, "so this is your first pregnancy?" I nodded my head and placed the prescription in my purse. The doctor reminded me to come back in three weeks. I floated out the door. Excitement had reached its level. My legs weren't carrying me fast enough. Tim was reading a book. He glanced up, "okay, well...ugh...well, Maggie what did the doctor say?" I blabbered, "Tim we are going to have a baby." Tim grabs me and spins me around. "Girl, we are going...baby...I...oh a baby...ugh...ugh, I am so excited." The nurse waved as we walked out of the door.

"Maggie, I am so lucky, beamed Tim. Let's get married right now." I replied, "now, hey, I am all for it, let's go." Everything began to happen so fast. First...finding out I was pregnant and then getting married in the same day. Tim opened the door for me; "come on girl, the judge is waiting. At that very moment I began following his orders. Tim suggested, "why don't you relax for a couple of hours." We left early that morning.

I didn't know where Tim was going as we drove. Finally he revealed the surprise...we are driving to New Orleans. The trip was a six-hour drive and I slept most of the time. Tim had relatives living in New Orleans. He wanted me to meet Uncle Buck. We checked into a motel as Tim understood my condition. I wish I could have wine and dine with him, after all, this was our honeymoon night. Tim convinced me by saying, "don't worry, girl. The rest of our life will be our honeymoon together. You go ahead and get in bed. I am going to call my uncle just to let him know that we made it here. Are you feeling okay?" I replied, "yes, so far I'm fine. But, I can't seem to get enough sleep. I know that's part of having a baby." Tim kissed me on the lips. "I love you so much. I don't want anything to ever happen to you."

We both slept like babies in each other's arms. The magic began all over again. We were caught up in the moment of passion. Tim expressed his love style though his splendid touch. His whispering words lavish my mind. He was everything I ever wanted in a man. Someone who can show love and affection too. He murmured in my ear, "baby, I love you. You are something else, girl. It can't get any better." I pushed Tim away. As I tried to get out of the bed, he caught me by the legs. "Hey, don't leave me," he beamed. We took our shower together.

We ate breakfast and took off for the city tour with Uncle Buck. We met him at Denny's restaurant. He was a nice person. We liked each other right away. He asked me a lot of questions. He took us on a boat ride down the Mississippi River. Later we ate at a Cajun restaurant. The food was almost too spicy for me. The men ate with gusto and I nipped with caution. Uncle Buck told hilarious stories about the New Orleans styles. I asked him about his family and he told us that his wife had left him for a white man. I apprehend the hurt in his voice. He retorted, "man I was a fool. I loved my wife so much I tried to give her everything in my power. Uh...um. That wasn't enough for her...you see...she wanted to get out of the house and work and make her own money. Yeah, as she called it." Tim asked, "how long have you been separated?" He uttered, "oh, no, we got a divorce last year. I couldn't stand what she did. You see, she begins working for this white couple. At first she was cleaning house. Later she claimed they wanted her to baby-sit late until the night. Well, to make the story shorter, they had an affair right under my nose. Yeah, it had been going on for the longest. The damn man didn't even have a family. He was living by himself." I felt sorry for Uncle Buck. He was so detracted towards his wife. You could sense that he still cared for her. I asked, "is she still living around here?" He turned to me with a sad look in his eyes. "I don't know, life goes on. I just take one day at a time."

Tim glanced at his watch..."man the time just flying by. We better get going if we want front seats at the Little Richard show." I shouted, "Tim, did you say Little Richard, oh my God." Tim beamed, "that's the surprise. I got tickets for you and Uncle Buck. Come on let's go." I was really surprised. We had a table at the very front. The show was a blast. Even Tim's Uncle Buck enjoyed himself. He met this nice lady and they hit if off at first sight. Tim and I just looked at each other. He whispered, "I thank God for you. Don't you ever leave me Woman." He kissed me on the nose. I murmured, "I love you too."

After the show we tried to get an autograph from Little Richard, but it was impossible to get near him. The security was too tight. We finally dropped Uncle Buck off to pick up his car. We departed to our hotel where we settled in to relax. The rest of the time in New Orleans was spent at the mall shopping for clothes. We shopped in the maternity department for several hours. I was so excited about gaining weight. I brought six maternity outfits for myself. I selected three wonderful suits for Tim. Making the long drive back home was terrible on my back. I was happy to be home. There is nothing like sleeping in your own bed.

I am six months pregnant with an additional thirty-five pounds to carry around. Tim is very excited about becoming a father. The baby is due in three months. We finally sold the farm and found a four-bedroom house in the suburban area, which was closer to the hospital. I decorated the entire house. We gave all of my old furniture to Mrs. Carter and another family that lived in the same area. I decorated one of the rooms for my baby. I was delighted about moving into my new home. I forgot all about the bad memories. We sold the farm to the Denton family from Georgia. They own a large herd of cattle. He purchased the farm for grazing land. Mr. Denton promised me he would not remove my grandparent's headstones from their graves.

Time passed. My awkward body maneuvered slowly around the house. One day as I was cooking dinner, I experienced the strangest feeling within my abdomen. The baby kicked me so hard I fell backward against the table I grabbed my stomach. "My god, what's happening to my baby?" I was frightened. I massaged my stomach slowly. My fingers sensed the warmth from within. "What's happening, I thought." I rushed into the bathroom and washed my face.

The heat in my stomach reminded me of the sensation of warmth I felt in my hands. I sat there for a moment contemplating my baby's next movement. I have been so busy with the new house; maybe I am just stressed from all the running around. I lay down on the sofa and closed my eyes. I thought about the children in my dream. Now I am going to be a mother myself. Suddenly, the baby stirred again but not with a hard kick...more like a flutter. I rubbed my stomach gently. I heard a voice whispered softly, "mother, mother." I frantically glanced around the room. Where was the voice coming from? No one was in the house. I calmed down. I heard the same voice again. Oh, my God, the voice was adverting from inside my womb. I thought I was dreaming. This can't be happening. I gently caressed my stomach. My baby moved quickly. I heard the voice again, "mother, mother. I answered spontaneously, "yes my dear, I am here. Mother is here." I waited for my baby to respond. The warmth gradually relinquished. I closed my eyes. Oh God, what does this mean? My baby is communicating with me before it is born. I remember the first time Tim and I made love, something strange happen. My child will be special. The secret power will be within his spirit. I no longer have the gift. The night my child was conceived my gift was given to him. I heard Tim at the door. I thought for a second about revealing my experience. This is not the right time I thought.

I opened the door. Tim stared at me, "what is wrong? You look like you had an arduous day." He kissed me while I tried to conceal my stimulate manner. "I feel like a giant

blimp, I murmured. Remember I am going to have a baby."
He rubbed my swollen belly. Tim eyes searched my face. He
responded, "are you sure, girl? You look like you just stole a
cookie from the cookie jar and got caught with the crumbs
around your mouth." One thing I learned about Tim, he
could always tell when I wasn't exactly telling the whole truth.
Tim took a bit of chicken chewing rapidly. He uttered,
"nothing could be more auspicious...today the rubber kettle
boiled over. I almost became a rubber maid ball." I chucked
so hard my belly jiggle like a bell. I responded, "well, I
wouldn't have to buy a ball for the baby. He could play with
'dear old dad' all the time.

  Tim worked for a rubber company that made all types
of hard rubber maid products. He was a conscientious
worker. Always influenced to go one more mile. Tim really
didn't have to work. We were financial set for the rest of our
life. Thanks to my parents. Tim was so energetic. I prayed
our baby would process some of his qualities and charms. He
touched my stomach as we sat at the table. "Wow, he
exclaimed, the baby sure is growing. I can't wait to hold him
in my arms." I was just as excited as Tim was. The phone
rang and Tim answered it. He passed the phone to me and I
recognized the voice on the other end. The voice replied,
"hello Mrs. Carter, this is doctor Bibliog. I need you to stop
by my office as soon as possible. Your test results are back. I
thought to myself, I was just in to see him one week ago. I
glanced around at Tim. "Baby, it's the doctor and he wants
me to come see him as soon as possible." I informed the
doctor I would be in tomorrow morning. I was just in a week

ago, I wonder if the test results show some type of problem."
Tim attested my state of mind. He replied, "Maggie, the
doctor has a reason for calling you back so soon. Now, don't
get that anxiety look on your face. Our baby is fine." Tim
eyes betrayed his sadness as he reached for me.

I rolled around in bed all night expecting to hear my
baby voice again. The next day Tim took off work to take me
to the doctor. We dressed quickly while both eyeing each
other. We were trying not to think of anything negative while
we took the hour long drive downtown. Upon arriving at the
doctor's office I sit down quickly. I was really anxious to see
the doctor. My hands began to sweat. Tim convinced me not
to worry, but he didn't know my secret. After sitting in the
setting room for ten minutes, which seemed like several
hours, the nurse assisted me into a room. I waited for the
doctor to come in. I thought to myself, "oh god," please don't
let anything happen to my baby. The doctor walked in
dressed in a crisp white lab coat. "Good morning Maggie, I
guess you are wondering why I called you back so soon." I
looked up with a wide eye expression. I uttered, "yes Doctor,
is anything wrong?" Doctor Bibliog sits down in a chair
besides me. He said, "now Mrs. Carter I don't want to
frighten you. The test I took last week shows your body's
toxic level is very high. "Maggie, your body is accumulating
lots of fluid which might affect your baby's health. I listen not
knowing what all of this meant. I asked, "what is causing so
much fluid?" The doctor explained to me how it happens to
some women due to the body not being able to flush out salt
from their system. After he explained what he thought was

causing the problem, he suggested that I be admitted into the hospital for some more testing. I gazed up at the doctor, "do you mean right now?" Doctor Bibliog quickly nodded, "well, I don't want to take a chance on your health nor your baby's health. He assured me that everything was going to be fine. I stayed in the hospital for two weeks. I was given test after test and put on a strict no salt diet. The food tasted awful and I lost weight.

The doctor allowed me to go home after promising him that I would not add salt to my food. I was glad to be home. Tim hired a housekeeper to help me around the house. I watched what I ate everyday. But, I still gained a lot of weight. My baby is growing fast. I have gained over sixty-five pounds. I am eight months pregnant and I visit the doctor every week. I feel and look like a big balloon. I can hardly walk. Tim took a leave of absent from work to be with me. The doctor and the nurses were amazed at the size of my baby. They checked me over and over thinking I might be having twins. But, each time the monitor only shows one heart beat.

Finally one evening, my water broke and Tim rushed me to the hospital. The doctor examined me...I was in labor. Tim called his mother. The pain began to come closer together and a lot more intensive as I lay on the bed. I twisted and turned but nothing eased the uncomfortable feeling. I wish my grandfather were here...I know he would cease the pain. Tim gripped my hands. My eyes glanced across the room. I prayed with all my strength that Grandpa would appear. My prayer was answered. Through the pain and sweat..., which seem like forever, I looked up at the ceiling. I couldn't believe my eyes. The blanket was hanging from the ceiling directly over my bed. I closed my eyes and relaxed. He's here, Grandpa's here. Tim kissed me lightly on my forehead, "Maggie, how are you feeling? Baby, it will soon be over." The pain vanished away. I open my eyes again and the blanket was no longer hanging from the ceiling. It was draped across my stomach.

CHAPTER 15

"THE ARRIVAL"

The nurse examined me and shouted, "the baby is coming. We better get her to the delivery room now." I touched my stomach hoping to feel the blanket. Even though it was there, no one could see it but me. The faded colors with ragged edges lay protecting me as a shroud of mystery encircling my body. The doctor asked Tim if he wanted to come into the delivery room. Tim was very nervous and remained in the waiting room. The doctor hadn't given me any drugs...however, I was not experiencing any pain. Thank you Grandpa, I thought. Tears flooded my eyes. The nurse wiped my face and she uttered, "I know you are in pain. It will all be over real soon, just relax." I thought with a smile on my face...there is no pain. The doctor uttered, "I see the baby's head. Okay Maggie, I want you to push." The words sounded like music to my ears. I pushed with all my strength and within seconds the baby was born. I opened my eyes slowly and behind the doctor and nurse, emerged Grandpa waving to me. I raised up from my pillow. The doctor and nurse eyed me strangely. I heard the doctor say, "oh my God." I yelled, "what's wrong with my baby?" The nurse answered, "Mrs. Carter you have a fine boy. Please just relax." She pushed my hair back from my face. The nurse quickly carried my baby out the room. Tim was delighted to hear the good news. He acted as if he was the one who had the baby. He tightly gripped my hand, "Maggie, we have a son. I am so happy it's over."

They moved me from the delivery room into a private room. All I could think about was seeing my baby. I forgot all about the presence of my grandfather in the room. I asked Tim if he had seen the baby, he nodded his head, "no not yet." I fell asleep for a few hours. When I woke Tim was sitting by my bed. The first thing came to my mind was my baby. I mumbled, "my baby, I want my baby." Two doctors entered my room and one of them walked over and looked at my chart. The oldest doctor approached my bed and said, "Mrs. Carter, I know you are anxious to see your baby. We must prepare you for something very phenomenal." I raised up in the bed..."what are you telling me? Is my baby dead?" Tim tried to calm me down. The doctor spoke in a soft voice and replied, "no Mrs. Carter, your baby is not dead. There is something we have to tell you. Your baby was born without eyes." I clustered the sheet and screamed, "no, no, that's not true." Tim rocked me gently in his arms. The doctor responded, "this is the first case we have ever had in this hospital. As soon as the baby is at least three weeks old, we will do other testing to find out what caused this to happen. So far this is all we can tell you right now. We will keep him in the hospital for awhile to make sure his system is free from toxic poison." "All I want is to see my son," I begged. "When can I see my baby?" The doctor responded, "they will bring your baby in soon." The doctors left my room.

Tim whispered, "we have a son." I lay there starring at the ceiling and suddenly I thought about the children without eyes in my dream. I murmured, "no Tim, they cannot use our child for experimental purpose." I wiped the tears from my eyes. Frantically, I tried to get out of bed. Tim held me down. He pleaded, "baby, baby, you can't get upset like this. They won't do anything without our permission." God help me, if they do." We didn't know what they were doing behind the closed doors. All I wanted was to see my baby and take him home with me.

My mind wandered back into the past. My nightmares were unfolding. Everything in my dream was coming true. My childbirth will baffle the doctor ability to understand the mystery of his beginning. I felt a relief in my mind as I pressed my head against Tim's chest. I beamed with joy. "Tim, it's okay, our son will not die until God is finished with him on this earth. His kind spirit will be like a light on the hilltop. He won't need eyes. God will be his eye. All he will need is the courage to live. Happiness filled my heart. I wanted my son in my arms. I ring the nurse and she replied, "yes, how can I help you?" I braced myself upon my pillow. "I want to see my son," I requested. The nurse answered, "they are on their way up." Tim boasted, "oh Maggie, we are going to see our baby." We eyed the door together. Finally the nurse peeped in the door. "Where is my baby," I asked? She responded, "just relax you will hold your baby soon." Within seconds the nurse stepped in the room holding my baby in her arms. I prepared myself. The moment had arrived. The nurse replied, "Mrs. Carter, here is your son. How are you this morning?" I couldn't speak...my mouth would not open. I nodded my head and she placed my baby in my arms. I quickly unwrapped the blue blanket from around his body. "Oh my God, I cried." My baby had no eyes. In the place for his eyes was just plain skin. His little round face was red as a beet. We stared at our son. Tim touched his little hand and boasted, "my son, he is so beautiful." "Yes, he is...he is perfect," I whispered. His hair was curled up around his little face. He looked so much like Tim. We sit gloating over our son as he lay in my arms. The love we had for our baby was so strong. To us, he was the most beautiful thing God could give us. The nurse stood beside the bed. She replied, "my, he is a beautiful baby. The doctor don't know what caused him to be born without eyes." I glowed with gratefulness. Because in my heart I knew my son was a special child. The nurse touched me on my shoulder, "Mrs. Carter, I must take your baby back to the nursery now." "But, I only had him for a little while, I insisted. Please, can we keep him just a little longer?" The nurse paused, "maybe, a few more minutes."

I held my baby close to my bosom and Tim put his arms around me. He whispered, "my son is everything I ever wanted. Honey, I love you very much." I kissed Tim, "I love you too." I attentively wrapped the blanket around his little body and placed my baby into the nurse's arms. She took our son back to the nursery. I relaxed on my pillow. My baby image locked in my mind. "Oh Tim, he is so beautiful. Our son is a gift from God." Tim asked, "what are we going to name our son?" Without hesitating I fleecy replied, "Sanato." Tim eyes widen, "where did you get that name from? Whatever happen to Junior?" "His name was selected for him before he was even born," I replied. "Sanato means without." Tim stared at me with a puzzled grin on his face and responded, "so you have been holding out on me. You knew all the time what you were going to name our son, didn't you Maggie?" I nodded, "yes, the name has been with me for awhile." Tim agreed, "well, Sanato sounds great to me." Tim didn't inquire how I came up with that name.

I stayed in the hospital for three days. We took the baby home with us. He was a perfectly healthy baby...born without eyes. He would live his life in darkness, I thought. The housekeeper helped me with my baby. Once we arrived, I spent all my time with my son. He gained weight so rapidly. I was amazed with the changes in his appearance.

◆

CHAPTER 16
"THE CHARACTER STAGES"

One night I was laying my baby in the bed, and as I laid him down I heard a gentle voice whisper, "mother." I listen quietly and again I heard the sound. My baby smiled as I touched his face. I moved away from the bed. His little head aimed in my direction as I paced around the room. I noticed that whenever I moved, he would turn his little head in that direction. I lightly stepped back from the crib. He can see me, I thought. I touched his innocent little face. A smile of contentment caught my sight. My anxiety ideas raced rapidly and I wanted to call out for Tim. Instead, I held his hands and was stunned by the warmth from his hands. I gradually pulled the blanket from around him. I gazed at my son as he lay there in his crib. "You are special, my son, I whispered. You have the gift."

The next day I revealed what had happen with our son. I took Tim into the baby's room. He couldn't believe what was happening. Sanato's head followed Tim as he moved around the room. After that night, Tim and I would come into the room and talk to our son. He loved him so much. Some nights I would wake and find Tim in the baby's room. Time passed very fast. Sanato is now eight months old. He began crawling when he was three months old. Now, he is walking. It's hard for me to keep up with him. He moves around so fast.

One morning I was feeding Sanato breakfast and a man knocked on the door. "Hello, Mrs. Carter, my name is Bob Hampton. I work at the medical center and would like to come in and talk to you about your son. "What about my son, I asked harshly?" "can I come in for a few minutes, " he replied. I invited him in. As he walked in he said, "I would like to discuss something with you about your son's problem. Your son was born without eyes. The hospital where he was born sent us his records. You see, we make parts for the body. As in your son's case, we could make him artificial eyes. Even though he won't be able to see, the man-made eyes would help his appearance as he grows up. A couple years back, there was a baby born with only one eye. The doctor made another one and it matched perfectly. You couldn't tell which one wasn't real."

I listened as Mr. Hampton talked. When he had finished, he passed me a business card. I paused not accepting the card. He continued, "I know you will need more time to discuss this with your husband." I resentfully responded, "no, I don't think I need any more time. You see Sir, my son don't need artificial eyes. God is his saver and eyes. I will not allow anyone to use my son for experimental use." Mr. Hampton uttered, "but Miss, just think of all the new technical skills we could introduce your son to." He passed me his business card again. I took the card, finally with a few more words. He walked towards the door.

The housekeeper called me suddenly from the baby's room. I dropped the card on the floor as I rushed into the room. The housekeeper was standing at the foot of Sanato's bed. She exclaimed, "watch this Mrs. Carter, your baby can see." I knew Mrs. France would soon discover his ability to see. As she moved from one side of the bed to the other, my baby followed her every move. I didn't know what to say to her. I really didn't want her to spread any rumors about my son. "Oh France, he only hear you moving around the room," I blabbered. She cried, "no, no, Mrs. Carter, watch this and don't say a word." She slowly picked her feet up and as she moved around the room...not making a sound, my son turned his head in her direction. She whispered, "see, I didn't make a sound at all. Your son can see me. I don't care what you think, he can really see." Mrs. France watched as I picked my baby up from the bed. I can imagine what was going on through her mind. A baby with no eyes, can see. I told her she could leave for the day. She gave me a suspicious glance as she left the room.

Neither Mrs. France nor the world will understand the gift my son process. The gift was passed down to him from my ancestors. The spirit will be within him. As long as he lives on this earth, he will be a mystery to all mankinds. Scientist will want to explore the knowledgeable tracts my son process. The strangest thing happens over the advancing months. France never spoke about my baby ability to see again. She would try all kinds of things with him. I heard her one-day calling Sanato her 'Miracle Baby.' Sometimes I would have to ask her to leave the baby's room to do other things in the house. Sanato loved France also. He would cry for her when she wasn't around him.

I hope his life will be normal. He will be a mystery to all mankinds. Scientist will want to explore the knowledge of his ability. Summer is almost over and Sanato is one year old. He can open the doors and walk around the house all by himself. We sit and watch him for hours as he moves about from one room to another. It's a mystery to see him walking around without eyes. Yet, he plays with his toys and talks to his pet kitten, curly. The first time I heard him call me mother, the recurrence of the dream came back so clearly in my mind. I remember the children in my dream calling me mother. My son exhibited a high degree of intelligence for his age. Coloring in his books is one of his favorite hobbies, other than eating spaghetti. He will blow each string of spaghetti before he eats it. One day on his fourth birthday, Sanato rubbed my face and touched my eyes. "Mama, what are these," he asked? "They are called eyes...this is how Mama can see you." Sanato rubbed his face and said, "Mama, why don't I have any eyes like you and daddy?" My heart began to beat faster and faster. I never told Sanato that he was born different. I wanted to wait until he was older. I held my hand up to Sanato's face, "baby, you have eyes, but no one can see them. God is your eye. He helps you to see." "Look, can you see Mama?" He hesitated with a big smile on his face. "Yes, I can see you Mama," and then he ran off to play with his kitten.

Three weeks after Sanato fifth birthday, a car hit his kitten. I heard the sound and ran outside. Curly lay very still. I was sure she was dead. I sat there on the ground with my son as he caressed Curly. She began to move her legs and finally her eyes opened. Sanato shouted, "Mama, Mama, Curly is okay now." After that day, Sanato never asked questions anymore. It was as if he knew what he was born to do. I would stand back and watch him. Sometimes baby birds would fall from their nest and he would always be around to save them. I would give a cheerful smile.

One evening Tim and Sanato were outside together. Tim was mowing the lawn and Sanato was playing with his ball. Tim stepped on a sharp object that almost cut off his toe. He screamed out in pain. "Sanato, go get your mother." Hearing his father scream in pain, Sanato rushed to his aid. He quickly pressed his father's toe back together. The bleeding stop instantly. Tim was in a state of shock. He had never seen anything like that in his life. He lay on the ground with his mouth opened in a surprisingly manner. Sanato explained what had happen. Tim groaned, "Maggie, our son has the power to heal just like you. Remember when you healed my mother? Look at my toe, it was almost cut off. How long have you known about this?" "Oh, I've always known in my heart from the day that he was conceived in my womb that he would have a special gift. The gift that he gives so freely to everyone." I commented with a gleam of proud in my voice. I told Tim about Sanato's kitten and the birds. Tim was stunned at the news. "My son has a miraculous gift. I don't understand the power, but, I thank God each day."

One afternoon we were watching television and suddenly the channel changed while the remote control was lying on the table. We stared at Sanato. He began to grin in a mystify manner. He could change the station on the television without the remote. We were amazed at the things our son could do. We learned something new about his ability everyday. Throughout the five years, he has shown leadership characteristics.

Sanato is almost school age now. It is time for us to begin looking around for special eye covers. We made an appointment with one of the eye specialist in town. They had talked with us about making the glasses for our son. The eye covers are very expensive. However, we don't mind the cost, just whatever it takes for our son to live as normal as possible. The specialists decided to come to our house to meet Sanato. Two specialists came to our house the following week. They measured Sanato's head. They displayed many different kinds of styles to choose from. As we looked through the books...Sanato pointed at one pair of eye covers that he liked. He blurted out; "I want this pair, Mama, the silver one." The specialists goggled at us with an astonishing impression on their faces. One of them said, "oh...that 's wonderful. He's pretending to see the pictures. Sanato responded, "sure, I can s__." I grabbed my son by the hand. "No son, let's not tell our secrets." He quickly agreed, "okay, but Mama please get the silver and black ones." The specialist gaped at my son. He replied, "yes, you sure guessed the right colors...that's really weird." Tim assured Sanato that he would get the silver and black shades. We completed the order form and paid one-half of the total price. I want to see the product before I pay the total cost.

After the specialists left, Sanato sauntered up to his father and retorted, "that man was so fat and his breath smelled really funny. I didn't want him to measure my head." Tim laughed and said, "Maggie, did you hear our son?" I agreed with Sanato...the fat guy's breath was too much for me.

We brought Sanato a new bicycle for his sixth birthday. It took three months before the company shipped Sanato's glasses. He was very excited about his eye covers. Now he can go out and not have people staring at him. Tim opened the box, but not fast enough for our son. He ripped the box open quickly. Tim helped Sanato try on the shades. He took off on his bicycle...padding as fast as he could go. We stood on the lawn and watched our son. Tim kissed me lightly. "Baby, look at our son, the world belongs to him now." Sanato shouted to us as he passed, "I'm Superman, I'm Superman." Tim watched as the arrogant father. I folded my arms, as I was pleased too. Sanato can go to school without the other children making him feel like an outcast. Tim said, "oh, let him play …in a couple of weeks he will be in school."

The weeks passed by quickly. I began searching for a school closer to our home. There were several schools in the neighborhood. For some reason I choose a school three miles away from our house. Well, for one reason, the school had been newly remodeled. I made an appointment to enroll Sanato in the first grade. He was very thrilled about going to school. I brought all new clothes for him. He was very big for his age…only six years old and wearing sizes for a twelve year old. His shoes were size 9. Tim and I were not very tall. Sanato took his height after his great grandfather.

On the first day of school, Sanato appeared a little nervous. But, I assured him that everything would be okay. Sanato wore his special glasses all the time. They were designed like regal dark shades. My son is six years old now and very intelligent with a much more matured mine. He is awfully excited about going to school. His glasses are designed with wide frames to hide the place where his eyes should have been. The glasses are special made to fit tight around Sanato's head. The company that manufactured the regular motor cycle helmets designed Sanato's shades. The glasses were very expensive. We paid a lots for the first two pair. The price didn't matter to us. The glasses gave our son a greater advantage in the future. The straps on Sanato's glasses were adjustable to his head. The eye covers were important because they would allow him a chance to live a normal life.

As we walked down the hallway, I noticed other parents registering their kids. Several of the kids stared at Sanato glasses, but for only a brief second. I walked over to the desk and one of the teachers gave me some forms to fill out. She asked, "what grade will is your son in this year?" I responded, "oh, this is his first year." She glanced at my son. "My he is a big boy for his age. How old is he?" Other people began to stare at us. I told her he was six years old. I had to show her his birth certificate for proof of his age. I smiled at her as she passed me the birth certificate back. I noticed how the other parents were looking at my son. They began to whisper among themselves. I pretended not to hear them, but of course, it was hard not to hear what they were saying. One of the parent asked, "my God, he's only six, he looks twelve." Sanato began to feel very uncomfortable. He pulled my hand and requested, "Mama, let's go home." He pushed his glasses closer to his face. Whenever Sanato felt uneasy about a strange place or person, he would always pushed his glasses closer to his head. To make sure no one could see under his glasses. After I completed all the forms, we waited to talk with the teacher. Sanato loved the idea of going to school. He was only afraid of being different from the other kids.

"You must do things you

think you can not do."

E.R.

CHAPTER 17

"THE SPECIAL BOND"

After I registered Sanato in school, we passed the principal's office. The name on the door read, Mr. Curtis Anthony Lewis. The last name rung a bell in my head. I have heard that name before, I thought. Sanato and I waited near the door until the other ladies finished speaking with the principal. Finally, the principal invited us into his office. I glanced at the picture on his desk of a black woman with three mulatto children. Mr. Lewis asked, "what can I do for you today?" "I'm here to register my son in school. He's anxious to meet the principal," I explained. "Well, I'm sure he is going to like it her. I have three kids myself," he boasted while pointing to the picture on his desk. Mr. Lewis asked, "did you grow up around here?" "Yes, I responded. I am from Basville County." He uttered, "you know my parents own some land out that way somewhere." He glanced over Sanato register forms while staring at me with inquisitive eyes. "Yes, I replied. I live about three miles from the school." Mr. Lewis peeped over his eyeglasses. "You look so familiar to me. What is your name?" I thought for a second...this couldn't be the Lewis that I worked for. I uttered faintly, "Maggie Johnson-Carter." Mr. Lewis dropped the papers on the floor. "Maggie, Maggie," he exclaimed, "are you the same Maggie that baby-sit me and my little sisters?" "It can't be you...is it really you." I cried out, "Little Junior, no it can't be true." I can't believe this." Mr. Lewis embraced me. "You know those big brown eyes of your still looks the same. Remember when you first came to the farm? I asked you if that color on your skin would wash off." I uttered, "I remember that very well. You were very young." He continued, "Mama told me what my father tried to do. I always wonder what happened to you?" Mr. Lewis looked around at Sanato...now this is your son? He's a mighty fine looking fellow." "Thank you. Mr. Lewis it is wonderful to see you again." He interrupted, no Maggie, don't call me Mr. Lewis, call me Junior." Whatever happen to Bertha," I asked? Mr. Lewis pointed down the hall; "she is right around the counter. Bertha is our fifth grade English teacher. Go on down there and surprise her." "He continued, "I can't believe you are standing here in my office. It's been along time." "Well Junior, I laughed at the sound of his name, "I don't want to take up any more of your time...I know you are a busy man." Mr. Lewis grinned, "you know it sounds good to hear that name. No one calls me that anymore." Sanato faintly reacted, "I have new eyeglasses. Do you like them?" Mr. Lewis gaped at Sanato's eyeglasses, "why yes," he exclaimed, they are very becoming. I haven't seen any like that before." He walked over to my son, "let me see them." Sanato jumped back and shouted, "no, no. Mama said, I must wear them all the time." I tried to explain to Mr. Lewis why my son reacted so strongly. I made up something about Sanato eyes being sensitive to light, which required him to wear his eyeglasses at all times. My son paced behind me holding on to his eyeglasses. He didn't want Mr. Lewis to see his face. He was afraid he wouldn't allow him to go to school.

I embraced my son...hoping to calm him down. He wanted to go to school more than anything. Mr. Lewis accepted my answer without any questions. He continued the conversation about his family. The phone rung and Mr. Lewis answered it. "Maggie its good to see you again. I hope I will see your son in school. Be sure to go by and visit Bertha."

I closed the door behind me as we walked down the hall to Bertha's room. Sanato asked, "Mama, do you know the principal?" "Yes, son, I baby-sit him and his little sister many years ago. I worked for the family until on day Mr. Lewis tried to...rap...he...I...Realizing I hadn't told Sanato about what happen on the farm, I hesitated. Now was not the time. "Come on let's go and surprise Bertha." We walked toward her door. She was sitting in her wheelchair just like the first day I saw her on the farm. Only, she has grown up now. Her eyeglasses were still very thick with black rims. Bertha was hurt in a car accident when she was just a baby, which left her paralyzed from the waist down. I remember her voice as I stared at her wheelchair. I knocked on the door and Bertha turned around. She was sitting at her desk reading. "Hello, I'm looking for Bertha Lewis." Bertha glanced up from her book, "oh my God, it is you. Maggie, Maggie, is that really you?" Tears webbed in the corner of her eyes. "Yes, Bertha, this is what's left of Maggie." Girl, it's been a long time." She recognized me instantly. "Maggie I can't believe you are here. Now who is this young man?" Looking at Sanato through her thick glasses. "This is my son, Sanato. He will be in the first grade this year." Bertha gazed at my son. "Sanato, that is a beautiful name. I heard that name somewhere before. I think it means without or something of that nature." Sanato little heart stopped beating at the very sound of her words. I could feel it in his grip as he clinched my hand. Bertha replied, "Maggie, you still look the same. I'm sure you already met my big brother up front." "Oh yes, I uttered, I was surprise I didn't recognize him. He looks so distinct." He was so skinny when he was a little boy. We sit gossiping about old times. I remember the first day I saw Bertha. I was only 14 years old. We had a special bond from the very first day. Bertha cried, "yes, you were my only friend. You played with me even when you had to clean up the house for Mama. You never forgot about us. Mama informed me how my father was killed. I never understood what happened to you." "Oh Bertha, it's not a good time to talk about that now. I have my son with me. Maybe, one day we can chat about the pass. That's what it is...it 's all over with. I want to remember the good times I had on the farm with you and Junior."

Bertha wiped her eyes while rolling her chair around towards Sanato. She declared, "that name goes well with your personality. I remember it means without fear. Sanato smiled and his fingers relaxed in my hand. He approached her, giving her a big hug. She pushed Sanato's curly hair back from his face. "Boy, I really like those eyeglasses. You will be the only one in the school with that style. She touched his hand, you will love it here." Bertha glanced around, "Maggie, I want you to meet my nieces. They are the most precious things in the world. I am not able to have kids, so I adopted my brother children as my own." "Why Bertha, that's a wonderful thing to do. You have so much love to give to the children." Bertha pulled out a picture of a little boy about six years old from her desk. "This is one of my student. His mother and father were killed in a car accident. I am thinking about adopting him. His name is Ron Franklin. He is my baby." I looked at the picture, "why he is a very handsome little boy." He lost both of his legs in the car accident. I fell in love with him the first time I saw his little fragile body," she explained.

I looked at my watch and the time had passed so fast. Sanato was drawing on the blackboard. I asked him to erase the board before we left. I promise Bertha that I would stop by and visit her some other time. Bertha tossed her hair back from her face, "wait Maggie, what are you doing everyday?" "I am just a housewife," I replied. My time will be free now that my son is in school." Bertha beamed with joys, "why don't you voluntary to help the children with special needs? Maggie, I know you will be great with the kids. Simply because you gave me hope. I never thought I could do any thing right until you taught me how to except myself the way I was and strive to do my very best with whatever life brings my way. Look at me, I went to college and received my degree. I think of this wheelchair as a pair of shoes, not as a handicap." She took my hand, "please...think about it, okay, Maggie?" I touched her hand, "oh Bertha, do you remember the first day I saw you? I was only 14 years old." Bertha nodded her head, "yes, we had a special bond from the very beginning. When I grew up my mother told us about my father's death. I never understood what happen that day. I know my father tried to do something bad to you. Please tell me what happen?" I walked around her chair, "Bertha that happened a long time ago. I hope that part of my life will remain in the pass. I only want to remember the wonderful times I spent with you." She quickly replied, "I understand," looking at Sanato with concerned eyes. She rolled her wheelchair around towards my son and asked, "what grade are you?" Sanato replied in a low voice, "I am first grade." Bertha glanced at me, "my, he's big for his age." Sanato kept his distance. He was afraid she would ask about his eyeglass. We said goodbye to Bertha. Sanato followed close besides me.

Sanato asked me, "Mama, how long have Miss Bertha been in a wheelchair?" I put my arms around my son. "Why, Miss Bertha have been in a wheelchair all of her life." Sanato ran back towards Bertha's room. I shouted, "Sanato, Sanato, where are you going?" I rushed behind him. Sanato pointed his finger towards Bertha. The wheelchair began to roll across the floor. Bertha screamed, "stop, stop." Sanato turned towards me. The chair stopped abruptly and hurled Bertha to the floor. She lifted up her head, feeling around for her glasses. I passed Bertha her eyeglasses. She was out of breath, pushing her glasses back on her eyes. "I don't understand what happened," she blabbered. "My chair...all...of a sudden...it just started rolling. What's happening, Maggie?" I glanced around at my son. He yelled, "get up Miss Bertha, you can walk." She looked so confused as she grabbed for her wheelchair. "I don't know what happened to that crazy chair. Did you see that, Maggie?" I nodded my head as I helped her back in her chair. Sanato shouted in the rear. "You don't need the wheelchair." Bertha stared with a worried tone in her voice, "Maggie, what is he talking about? Now you know I can't walk. I have been like this all my life. I can't walk, I can't do it."

I lifted up the footrest on her chair. Sanato grabbed my hand, "no Mama, let her try. Go ahead Miss Bertha, get up, get up he yelled." She wiped her eyes and placed both hands on her chair. Pushing with all her strength, she pulled herself into her chair. Bertha was so tense, sweat poured down her forehead. We watched as she braced herself to stand. She lifted herself up. The wheelchair rolled from under her. Bertha gazed me straight in the eyes. She pleaded, "Maggie, I feel so wonderful. It's my legs...the sensation is ripping through my bones...it feel warm...I mean something strange has happened." I replied, "Bertha, I am going to let go of your hands. Now if you think you can, you can Bertha...and if you think you can't walk...then you are right." Bertha expression changed to a serious degree, staring at her feet. She slowly pushed one foot out...then the other foot. Inch by inch, she moved. No doubt Bertha was walking. Sanato and I slipped away from her room. We could hear her shouting with joy as we walked down the hall. Mr. Lewis rushed down the hall to his sister's room. He shouted, "Bertha, Bertha, what is wrong?"

Sanato and I drove home. He was very quiet. "You were great today, my son. What you did for Bertha was a blessing." He replied, "Mama, I didn't do anything. Did you keep them when they were little like me?" I replied, "yes, they were younger than you. Mr. Lewis, Jr. was four and Bertha was three years. They were good children. Their mother was a very caring person. Sanato nervously twisted his hands together, "Mama, what about that man that hurt you." "Son, remember God has a way of guiding people back together. You see, Mr. Lewis paid dearly for his mistake." Sanato asked, "what happened to him, Mama?" "He was killed very mysteriously, I uttered. No one ever found out the real truth about his accident, but I know what happened." Sanato wanted me to tell him more.

As I drove up in the driveway Tim was waiting for us. Sanato jumped out of the car, "Daddy, Daddy, guess what, Mama registered me in school today. We met the principal and his sister. Mama, baby-sit for them when they were little." Tim smiled, "oh you ran upon the Lewis children at school." "Yes, I answered. He is the principal and his sister is a fifth grade teacher." Sanato hurried on to his room and turned his television on.

Several days later Mr. Lewis called and asked about his sister's recovery. He stated that his sister had said that an angel from heaven helped her. He came in the form of an old man with a blanket wrapped around his shoulder. Weeks passed, and finally one Sunday morning Bertha appeared at my door. I was delighted to see her. We chatted about what happened that day in her room. She replied, "I didn't realize you and your son had left my room. When I glanced up this old man appeared out of nowhere. He didn't say a word. He stared at me with kindness in his eyes." As she paced around the living room, she spotted my grandfather's picture on the wall. She hesitated in her tracts, gazing closer at the picture.

She stammered. "Maggie...ugh...this man, who is he," she asked while pointing at my grandfather. "Oh, that's a picture of my grandfather," I boasted. Bertha became very fascinated. "No, no, that's the same man I saw in my room. I know it was. He had the same kind eyes." I convinced Bertha that it was not my grandfather she saw. It was all in her mind. She didn't know how to explain what occurred. I told her that somethings are best left as mysterious concepts.

Bertha and I ate lunch together. It was wonderful to see her walking. Whatever inscrutable power made her walk would forever be a blessing in her life. She brushed her hair back with excitement in her voice. She uttered, "Maggie, during our life we encounter things we can't justify which leaves us in a daze. Without a doubt, miracles happen to those who believe in them.

One evening we received an urgent call from the principal's office. I bolted out the door wondering if something had happened to Sanato. When I arrived, the principal was waiting at the entrance. He spoke swiftly hoping to reassure me that my son was okay. As I approached the office, I saw Sanato sitting in a chair near Mr. Lewis' desk. I called out to him, "Son, what's wrong?" Sanato quickly answered, "Mama, Mama, I didn't mean to hurt him. Some of the students tried to pull off my eyeglasses." The principal interrupted, "Mrs. Carter, may I see you in private." We stepped outside the office. He spoke softly, "Mrs. Carter, your son didn't do anything wrong. It's the action that he took with the students that bothers me. You see during the struggle the students' head hit a concrete block. The boy was knocked unconscious. Now, Mrs. Carter I wouldn't stand here and tell you this if I hadn't seen it for myself. I sat quietly nodding my head as Mr. Lewis explained what happened. His face flushed as he pushed he glasses up on his nose. "Maggie, your son fell down beside the student. He elevated his head and called his name several times. The student vigorously sat up as if nothing had happen. All of the other students witnessed this strange occurrence. They knew something strange transpired. No one understood." I peeped at my son, with his head down; he pulled on his coat zipper. "Mr. Lewis, maybe sometimes things do occur beyond human comprehension which baffle our attempts to interpret," I uttered. I was hoping he wouldn't ask anymore questions. The principal answered, "Mrs. Carter, the students are very inquisitive about your son's eye cover. I am sorry...I mean eyeglasses. One of the students informed another that Sanato was born without eyes. Kids can be very rude. "Mr. Lewis," I replied in a firm tone, Sanato can see very well. Remember when I registered him in school, I clarified that his eyes were very sensitive to light. I hope we will not have this problem again with the students." Mr. Lewis gazed at Sanato. He replied, "well, you know Son, I haven't seen you without your glasses on either." Sanato pressed his glasses closer to his face as Mr. Lewis approached him. He apologized to Sanato for the trouble the students had caused. I spoke in an aggressive direct tone, "Mr. Lewis, my son don't have to show anyone his eyes." I patted Sanato on the shoulder. He murmured, "Mama, look, they tore my sweater."

I noticed the large hole in his sweater. I hastily uttered, "Mama will buy you another one."

Mr. Lewis promised me that this wouldn't happen again. School was not out, but I was allowed to take Sanato home. He grabbed his book bag and paced close besides me...so as not to hesitate any longer in Mr. Lewis' presence. We drove home. Sanato asked, "Mama, why am I different from the other children? They are always teasing me because my glasses are made different from anyone else in the school." They make me angry. I didn't want to hurt anyone. They wouldn't stop pulling on my sweater." I allowed Sanato time to release his angry. I replied, "son, you are a special child. You were born without eyes, yet you can see. It's a gift that was given to you before you were born. I don't understand how you are able to see. The mystery frustrates our attempts to expound the truth. Tim and I have tried to shield you from the public inquiries. The people are going to be inquisitive about your eye covers. I patted Sanato on the head. "Son, I love you very much. Learn to live with your disability. I pray for strength each day for you."

On the way home, we stopped by Denny's restaurant for lunch. All eyes turned towards us when we stepped in the door. Sanato acted very polite, although he was a little fidgety. When we were leaving the restaurant, Sanato strolled slowly behind me. Suddenly, plates began to dart through the air. Everyone screamed with confused conception. I guided Sanato out the door. "Why son, you didn't...are you responsible for that problem?" Sanato grinned showing his pearly white teeth. "That will teach them not to stare." I glanced back at the people sitting at the tables. Food and drinks were all over their clothes. I couldn't help but laugh at the expression on their faces. I guess they though a gust of wind caused the commotion.

As we drove home, Sanato replied, "I made those plates fly in the air." I questioned, "why did you do that, honey?" He replied, "because they stared at us all the while we were eating. Didn't you see them, Mama?" "Yes, I noticed them too, but son that wasn't right. Those flying plates could have hurt someone.

When we arrived home Tim greeted us at the door. He kissed me on the cheek, "hi, baby, is everything okay?" He grabbed Sanato's book bag, "hi Big Guy. How was school today?" Sanato answered, "hi Dad, school was fine, but...ugh...Mama had to come to get me today." Tim gazed at me, "what happen?" I explained the situation with the students and Tim listened attentively. Suddenly, he replied, "well, he did nothing wrong. Son, I am proud of you." Sanato uttered, "Dad, I didn't want to hurt anyone." Tim embraced Sanato, "you are special, my son, never harm anyone with your power." Sanato asked, "Dad, why do I have this special power?" Tim signaled me for an indicated answer. He stammered " I ...ugh...well...I ...don't understand why you have the special gift. Maybe, the answers will be revealed to us one day."

Many questions were asked concerning Sanato's eye cover. As he grew up and we would always convey that his eyes were very sensitive to light and that he needed to wear shades all the time. For Sanato's eight birthday, we bought him a red bicycle. He loved to ride his bicycle up and down the street. Sanato reminded me of my grandfather in so many ways. His skin was a light bronze color. His hair was very dark with thick curls hanging loose around his ears. Sometimes when I looked at my son without his eye cover, I could foresee the children in my dream. I had recurrent dreams before Sanato was born. The children could see, yet they had no eyes. They were very happy children just like Sanato. I knew my son had the gift to heal. He had power that I myself didn't understand.

As the months and years passed by, our son grew older as did Tim and I. We opened a trust fund for Sanato and willed all of our procession to him. Sanato made all A's in his classes. The teachers gave him several awards for his achievement. The house was filled with trophies and certificates. He made lots of friends...the girls didn't mind his eye cover. As a matter of fact, they thought he was just a regular guy wearing cool shades. Some of the other boys bought big sunglasses to imitate Sanato's look. He had so much love to give. We assured him of our love and instructed him to love himself and respect the rights of others. He enjoyed making other people happy. He would ask us for money to give to another student who needed shoes or a coat. He never ate at home alone. There were always several students over for dinner everyday.

Years passed by quickly. On Sanato's seventeenth birthday, we brought him a sports car. He loved cars and nothing could have made him any happier. He looked so handsome riding around with the top down. His eye cover appeared more like jazz shades. Sanato wheeled all of his friends from school. One day after school, he introduced us to his special friend. Her name was Gail. She was an extremely shy, long legged girl with ebony hair. Her skin was the color of homemade molasses. She smiled and said, "hi, my name is Gail." Her teeth were white as snow. Tim and I welcomed her to our home. Tim turned to Sanato, "son...where did you find such a beautiful lady?" Sanato beamed, "she sit right in front of me in my English class. Not only is she beautiful, she is smart, too." Gail didn't talk very much the first time she came over to meet us. Later, she became Sanato's special friend. He spent a lot of time with her. We saw less and less of him each day.

As months passed, I wondered about Gail's true motive for dating my son. She didn't seem to mind Sanato's eye cover. Maybe it was his money or his red sports car that made her so fascinated with him. The thoughts stirred in my head each time I saw her with him. One evening as we cooked outside, Gail stated openly, "Mrs. Carter, your son and I have been friends for several months. I have never seen him without his shades on. I wonder sometimes, what color are Sanato's eyes." Just as I began to respond to Gail's question, Sanato walked up behind Gail. He boasted, "hey, you want to know what color my eyes are? They can be any color you like, blue...green...or... He tickled Gail behind her neck and she bounced with excitement. He rubbed her neck as she lurched out..."oh Sanato, you are so funny. I know you can change the color of your eyes with contact lens." I smiled at Sanato...it was our secret.

Tim and I promised we would never reveal the truth. After Tim finished cooking, Gail helped set the table. She exhibited a happy smile on her face. Nodding towards Sanato she said, "your son is too much. I have never met anyone like him before. He's so...well, I mean, he's too decent to be genuine." I touched her hand gently. "My dear, you will never meet anyone like him...not ever." Gail grinned as if I was joking with a silly look on her face. She was not sure of the power behind my statement.

The friendship between Gail and Sanato grew into a serious relationship. At least that's how she projected it to be. Something just wouldn't completely permit me to trust Gail. A feeling that only a mother could understand, or maybe I was wrong about her. One night after Sanato returned home from a date with Gail, he asked for permission to go away for the weekend. Tim glanced at me. I nodded my head expressing a favorable gesture. He was a junior in high school and very mature. We didn't see any reason why he couldn't go. Sanato shrugged, "Mama?" I answered, "yes, you can go." He addressed his father and Tim replied, "sure it's fine with me. Are you hanging out with your friend, Gail?" Sanato uttered, "yes, she is cool to." Tim replied, "look like you are an inseparable couple." Sanato strolled around the room with his hands in his faded jeans pocket, prancing around like a proud stallion. "Oh, yes...ugh...one day I just might marry that girl. He grinned from ear to ear...ugh, I think I am in love."

Sanato was our only son. We were indulgent parents not allowing Sanato space to be himself, to live his life to the fullest. Later Tim and I discussed the trip. We made sure Sanato had everything he needed for the weekend. I was a little fidgety, but surprise at how Tim managed to hide his feelings. We were both over protective of our son. As the weekend approached, Sanato washed his car over and over. He bought enough new clothes for three weeks. On Saturday morning Sanato loaded his things into his car. We waved good-by as he drove away. Tim grinned, hugging me closely. "There goes our boy." I clinged to Tim's arm. I prayed that everything would go well. After Sanato left, we tried to keep busy. I began wandering around the house picking up things. I tried not to worry about my son.

The next day Tim and I went to church. Everyone asked, "where is Sanato?" He always attended service with us. After service, Tim and I went home. He was exceptionally quiet. I knew he was concerned about our son. After dinner we blabbed about Sunday services. Finally Tim asked, "what time is Sanato coming home?" I replied, "around midnight, I think." Tim glanced at his watch, "well, he got about five more hours." Tim relaxed on the sofa. I had this weird feeling as if someone else was in the room with us. I stepped over to the window. The stars were bright. Tim raised up, "Maggie, what's wrong?" I couldn't explain the feeling. But I had felt this way before. When my grandfather's presence was in the house. Tim replied, "you are acting very jittery...come on over here." He put his arms around me. He continued, "I know you are concerned about Sanato. He will be okay." I answered, "well, yes...but, it's something else. I really do miss my son." Tim replied again, "Baby, he will be fine." Eyeing his watch, "okay...we have about three hours to wait." He beamed, "come on let's watch a movie." I picked up the remote control and scanned through the channels. To my surprise, a new movie was on. I relaxed in Tim's arms.

We didn't realize how fast the time had passed until we heard Sanato's car pulled up in the driveway. I jumped up. Tim pulled me back down on the sofa. He whispered, "Maggie, calm down." We don't want our son to think we were sitting here waiting for him to come home." I slowly sat back down on the sofa. The door opened and Sanato pranced in with a big smile on his face. "Hi Mama...Daddy, you guys miss me?" We reached for Sanato at the same time. Tim answered, "did we miss you, boy." "I thought I was going to have to take your mom to look for you." I replied, "oh no, I wasn't worried at all." Sanato uttered, "I had a wonderful time. We spent the weekend at Camp Three Height." He clang to my arm, "Mom, you and Dad must come with me the next time." Tim inquired, "what did you do out in the woods?" Sanato rubbed his stomach. "Ugh...ugh...man, I ate a lots of fish and shrimp." I asked, "did your friends Maxi and Jeremy go?" Sanato blabbered with a slight grin on his face. "Yes, and so did their girlfriends." Tim helped Sanato bring his things inside. I shouted, "hey guys, it's getting late." Sanato, do you have to go to school tomorrow?" Sanato retorted, "no Mom, tomorrow is Teacher's meeting day. "Hey...you know I thought about staying over another night...but, I knew you guys would be worried sick." Tim replied, "yes your mother was a little concerned." Sanato took his suitcase to his room

and closed his door. He turned on his radio and his music
agitated me. He played ear-splitting music all night.

Nothing is so embarrassing as watching someone do
something that you said couldn't be done.

S.E.B.

◆

CHAPTER 18

"THE MESSAGE"

The next morning the sun sparkled through the window. The sound of Tim taking a shower woke me up. I raised up in bed, thinking maybe, I will surprise him by cooking a full breakfast before he left for work. As I entered the kitchen, Tim shouted, "I already had a cup of coffee...I need to get to work early." Tim kissed me again. "Baby, you sure are looking sexy this morning. I hate to leave you, but you know I must go to work. I am not the one to live off no woman, especially my wife." I was very proud of my husband. I kissed him behind the neck. His fingers gently fondled my ringlets. My face flushed from his body heat. Tim pushed me back, breathing down heavily on my face. He whispered, "Girl, if you keep this up, I don't think I will go to work at all." I kissed him again and he reacted, "Girl, if I don't get out of here, we are going to end up back in bed...Baby...I ...ugh...I enjoy working. Taking care of you is important. I know we have plenty money. I would be less of a man if I sit around and use your money." He glanced at his watch, "okay, okay, I am out of here." He kissed me again, patting me on my rear end. He whispered in my ear, "I will pick up where I left off tonight...okay?" With a boyish grin on his face, he hurried out the door and speeded away in his new pick-up truck. I watched him as he drove away. Tim looked so handsome driving his new truck. His birthday was two weeks ago and I

brought him a new red truck. He was totally surprised.
Sanato parked the truck in the back yard. I insisted that Tim
take out the trash. Tim fussed for a few minutes. He said he
wondered why Sanato hadn't taken out the trash earlier. I
gave Tim a gawky look. Finally, he grabbed the bag...while
being exhausted from working all day and dashed out the
door. The truck was parked under the big oak tree. Sanato
was sitting in the truck. He shouted, "happy birthday,
Daddy." Tim's agitated expression faded away with an
ecstatic tone as he yelled, "what, a new truck? I can't believe
your Mama. She is wonderful." Sanato boasted, "come on,
let's go for a ride around the block." I stated, "man, if you
hadn't taken that trash out I was going to take that truck
back to the truck dealer." Tim embraced me, "oh Baby, it's
beautiful. How did you know I wanted a new truck?" I
replied, "well, the one you have is always breaking down. You
have had that truck for many years. Remember I gave you
that old truck the night we found the secret tree?" Tim
rubbed his head, "yes, I will always remember that night."
Sanato looked at both of us seriously, like...what are you two
talking about?"

   We never told Sanato about the money we found in the
woods. Tim laughed, "oh, what a trick your Mama played on
me in the woods before you were born." Sanato uttered,
"ugh...ugh... tell me more." Tim insisted, "come on son, let's
take that ride." As I walked back towards the house, I saw a
shadow of a man in the window. I stood there for a second
while my eyes were fixed on the window. "Oh...I thought...I
saw a shadow. Maybe, it's my grandfather. He's gone, I

thought as I looked around the room." I noticed a note on the table which read, "a new life begins and a life ends." I read the note over and over again. What does this message mean? Suddenly, the note vanished right before my eyes. Will I have another baby, I thought? No, I can't have another baby...not at my age. I was in deep thought when I heard the door open. I turned around quickly to see Tim and Sanato standing in the doorway. Tim boasted, "wow, you looked like you were expecting someone else. I shrugged, "oh no, I was just waiting for you guys to return." Sanato replied, Mama are you okay?" I answered, "yes, I am fine.

"Tim do you like the new truck?" Sanato knew something was wrong. He had that inner sense when something was not right with me. He paced the floor and I tried to convince him that everything was okay. Tim kissed me, "Baby, that truck sure does drive smooth." We drove around longer than I expected. I placed a luscious kiss on Tim's lips, "it's getting late, Honey...I think I am going to bed." Tim replied, "sure baby, go ahead and I will be in soon." "Good-night," I uttered.

My perception was not there. I pondered with the message...was this note for me or for Sanato? I repeated the words in my head over and over. "A new life begins and a life ends." I set on the side of my bed, thinking. I can't have another baby. After Sanato was born, I had surgery. I closed my eyes but was unable to sleep. I tossed and turned all night long. The next morning, Tim left for work as usual...running with a cup of coffee in his hand. I waved good-by as he drove off. I went into the bedroom noticing myself in the mirror. My hair was turning gray. I pulled my hair back from my face. I am looking more and more like my grandmother as the years passed. I thought about what my grandfather would say, "time brings about a change and tim stands still for no one." Sanato is a senior in school. It seen like only a few years ago when the nurse laid my son in my arms. The sound of glass breaking in the kitchen brought m back into the present. I hurried into the kitchen and Sanato was picking up glass off the floor. He murmured, "good morning, Mama, I broke a glass. I'm sorry, I didn't mean to wake you." "Oh, you didn't wake me. I was already up. Let me fix you some breakfast," I insisted. Sanato responded, "I ate a bowel of cereal. Would you like something?" "No, I'm fine," I said as I sipped on my cup of coffee.

I asked Sanato to drive me downtown. I wanted to bu new curtains for my room. I was colorblind and he could helped me with the color coordination for my room. Sanato quickly answered, "yes Mama, I will be happy to drive you. We are going in my car, right?" I answered, "sure we can go in your car." Sanato loved to show off his sports car especially when he is driving his father and me around town Tim and I didn't mind riding with our son. Sometimes he drove too fast. He would say, "come on you guys, loosen up little bit. Let your hair blow in the breeze."

We talked about the good times on our way into town When we reached the intersection, the traffic was going very slow. Several cars had stopped ahead of us. "What's going c up there" I yawned after a brief nap? Sanato pulled over on the side of the road and opened the door. "Look Mama, someone is lying on the ground. I think there's been an accident." He ran towards the crowd while looking back over his shoulder. He shouted, "Mama stay in the car." I waited a few minutes while becoming restless due to the heat. I grabbed my purse and began walking towards the accident. People were standing around looking as I approached the scene. I noticed a big truck had flipped over on top of a car. The emergency team arrived. They asked everyone to move back. I was standing there shaking. The lights reminded me of the night Dan was killed. I glanced around. Where is Sanato? I knew my son was here but I couldn't find him. I thought, "where are you?" my eyes searched the crowds. No Sanato. I shouted his name out loud and everyone stared at me. With all the excitement, I lost one of my earrings. I decided to go back to the car. I glanced up and Sanato was sitting in the car with a weird look on his face. Bloodstains were all over his clothes. I opened the door quickly. Sanato nervously confronted me, "Mama, I tough I told you to stay in the car." I was totally out of breath. I stutter, "where...ugh...where...ugh were you? I was looking for you." Sanato insisted dryly as if he was not himself, "Mama, please buckle your seat belt." As he drove, I sat anxiously waiting to hear about what was happening. Sanato replied, "Mama, I was inside the ambulance. When suddenly this old blanket floated over the lady and her daughter. No one could see the blanket but me. I guess they couldn't see me either. The blanket floated down slowly, like a cloud heavy with rain and shielded their bodies. The emergency team frantically worked. No one said a word to me." I answered, "well, I didn't see you myself." Sanato replied, "oh, you didn't?" He searched my face with his inquiring mind. He replied, "you know something, Mama, I felt as if I was apart of the cloud, when I was in the ambulance...wow...it was real weird."

"I wonder sometimes if we were meant to be at that particular spot. You know everything happens for a specific reason in our lives. My son, you are a part of the mystery of the blanket just as I am a part of you." Sanato nodded his head. "So I am right," I stated..."yes, my dear, we were there at the right time." I stared ahead as Sanato pulled into the driveway. He opened the door for me. I put my arms around him. He asked, "my great grandfather is dead but he seems so real. I know there is a mystery. The blanket floated around inside the ambulance like a 'halo of mercy.' " I replied, "a mystery indeed...that's how I remember my grandfather."

Tired from all the stress, I quickly relaxed on the sofa. I noticed my son looking at the pictures on the wall. He frowned, "ugh...yeah, that was my great grandfather I saw all right. He looked the same as these pictures." I passed the photo album to him. The pictures caught Sanato's attention. I closed my eyes and relaxed my head against the soft pillow. I thought, "so my grandfather appeared to Sanato for the first time. The whole day began to fall in place in my mind. I didn't need new curtains. I had just replaced all of my windows with new ones just a few months ago. Sanato and I were on a mission. Our job was to be there at the time of the accident. Maybe not me, but making sure my son was there. Sanato learned a lot about how great love abides. Whatever we implant in our mind makes us believe in the unknown, or maybe what the eyes cannot se. The paramedic stated in the news how hard they worked to save the people's lives. I didn't see my son. He had to be invisible, I thought. Grandfather had used his power to make an 'angel of mercy' come to rescue those hurt in the accident. That explains how Sanato was able to return back to the car without me seeing him.

♦

CHAPTER 19
"THE NEW FAMILY"

I laid my head back on the sofa. My, this day had been a day to remember. My lids began to feel heavy. As I closed my eyes, the doorbell rang. I hesitated for a few minutes...hoping Sanato would answer the door. I quickly remembered that he had gone out with Gail. I rubbed my eyes trying to focus my sight on the doorknob. I opened the door and Mrs. Green framed the door with her granddaughter, Bonnie. I replied, "how are you Mrs. Green? It's so good to see you again." We embraced each other. Mrs. Green nodded her head towards Bonnie. "She is a lucky little girl, I know you did all you could to help her that day." Mrs. Green's facial expression became more intense. I asked, "how did this happen with Bonnie? I mean her recovery." Mr.

Green answered, "well, it was the strangest thing. I still don't understand what transpired. I am just happy about everything." I asked, "was anyone else involved in helping Bonnie to walk?" Her eyes widened as she took a deep breath. Shaking her head, she answered, "one day I was walking from the store not very far from home. Bonnie didn't feel up to going with me. This old man appeared on the other side of the street. I didn't recognize him as someone from the neighborhood. He seemed like a very pleasant person. He wandered over and spoke to me and I politely greeted him back. He grinned with a big smile as if he knew me." I nodded my head as I listened to Mrs. Green's story. "Would you like some tea?" I rushed to the kitchen and poured Mrs. Green and Bonnie a glass of tea. I dashed back to hear the rest of her story. She gulped down a big swallow of tea and wiped her mouth with her hand. She responded, "ugh...ugh...that's cold and good, just the way I like it." I didn't want the conversation to end. I asked, "what did this old man do after that. I think you were saying he smiled at you as if he knew you." "Well, she continued, he said, Lady...why are you looking so disturbed?" I answered without even thinking, "life is hard sometimes, Sir." He replied with a twinkle in his eyes, "life is a journey and each breath of air we take for granted is a gift of mercy." We continued to walk together and all of a sudden, he stopped and lifted the blanket from around his shoulders and without another word, he ambled away." I exclaimed, "was it a very old raggedy worn out blanket?" Mrs. Green blabbered, "yes, yes, I wonder why he had a blanket around his shoulders. It was very hot that day." I was looking bewildered about the matter but did not want her to stop revealing what had happened. Then Bonnie interrupted and I said, "oh, I bet you are telling the story about the old man." "May I have some more tea?" I answered, "I will get you a glass of milk." Bonnie frowned, "okay, I will have a glass of milk." "I can't wait to tell you what that old man whispered in my ear." I dashed off to the kitchen again and poured a glass of milk and grabbed a couple of cookies from the jar. Mrs. Green replied, "Bonnie loves milk and cookies." I wanted to know the rest of the story. I commenced the conservation again. "Bonnie, what did the old man whisper in your ear?" She gulped down her milk and wiped her mouth with the back of her hand. She uttered, "ugh...ugh...when I first saw him he just appeared in the doorway. At first I was afraid, but he said, "don't be afraid. I am here to help you. I thought he was a gimpy old man who had wandered from the old folks home." Mrs. Green responded, "yes, he did look a lots like someone that might have been lost. I knew exactly who that old man was. I wanted to know what happen." Bonnie scowled, "wait Grandmother, let me tell Mrs. Maggie what he said." "What did he say Bonnie," I asked? She continued, "first, he pulled the blanket from around his shoulders and wrapped it around my legs. My legs began to feel very warm. Then he bent down and whispered, don't be afraid...get up and run like a running river." Bonnie took a deep breath while moving her hands around with a nervous twist. She replied, "that old man said, look down at your feet. When I looked up he was gone." Mrs. Green responded, "I tell you, he just disappeared

like a ghost. He frightened me really bad." Bonnie's eyes
widen with excitement. Taking a deep breath, she nodded, "I
got up from my wheelchair and began to run

My heart throbbed real fast in my mind. I pictured my
grandfather with a big grin on his face. Bonnie interrupted
my thoughts by placing the glass on the table. She replied,
"when my grandmother saw me, she fell to the ground as if
she had fainted." Mrs. Green uttered, with tears webbed in
her eyes, "the only words I could speak were...thank you
Jesus. My child can walk. I never saw that old man again.
You know, Mrs. Maggie, I think he was an 'angel' from
heaven. I looked around the house for him...even outside the
house. I called Mr....Mr....where are you? There was no
answer." I nodded my head, "well, peculiar things do happen
which we can't explain. I'm sure Bonnie's walking was a
miracle for your eyes to behold." Mrs. Green mumbled, "I will
always remember that old man's face. Oh, Mrs. Maggie, I
know you are tired of us blabbing about that old man."

Mrs. Green starts looking around in the kitchen. "My,
you have a beautiful home." "Let me show you the rest of the
house." Her face gave a glow of excitement. Suddenly Mrs.
Green yelled, "that's the man that healed my Bonnie. It's him
I am sure. His eyes had the same twinkle." She looked closer
and I stood back waiting for her to ask me about the man in
the picture. She stared at the picture for several minutes.
Mrs. Green turned to me, "Maggie, who is this man in the
picture?" I took a deep breath, "he's my grandfather. He died
many years ago," I answered. Mrs. Green exclaimed, "no, it
can't be. He's the man I met on the street that day. I know it

was him." I replied, "Mrs. Green, please sit down and let me explain. You see, my grandfather was killed many years ago." Mrs. Green began crying and shaking her head in disbelief. She wiped her eyes and placed her hands on the picture. She murmured, "thank you for healing my Bonnie." She turned to me, "Maggie, I will always be grateful to you. I am very happy I met you in the store. You transformed my life."

She gazed around for her daughter...thinking she was standing near her. She instantly began shouting, "Bonnie, Bonnie, where are you?" Bonnie yelled, "I am in here, Granny." We found her in Sanato's room admiring his shade collection. Bonnie stammered, "ugh...these are...real...cool glasses. There are so many different colors, who wear them?" I answered, "they belong to my son, Sanato." Mrs. Green picked up a pair of Sanato's glasses and inspected them. She asked, "why are they made like this, is he blind?" I responded, "well, I don't think you would understand what I am going to reveal to you. My son was born without eyes. Well, in a way he was born blind." Mrs. Green frantically sat down in a chair. She placed her hands over her mouth and murmured, "no eyes. My God, I know it must have been hard for you and your husband." I replied, reassuring her with a smile, "I knew my son would not have eyes before he was born." Mrs. Green's eyes widened with curiosity, "how in God's name did you know that?" I answered, "I had a dream before my son was even conceived in my womb. The children in my dream were calling me Mama. They had no eyes." Mrs. Green abraded her hands together in a nervous manner. I don't understand, you have a special gift. I thank God for you." I gave her a big hug. "I'm grateful too," I uttered.

I asked her about herself and Bonnie. She looked me firmly in the eyes. "Well, I lost my husband a couple of years age. Its just Bonnie and me." I didn't want to stare at Mrs. Green. She certainly had changed from the lady I met in the grocery store. She looked so old and worn out. Her hair was completely gray. The wrinkles in her face implied a hard life. "Where are you living now," I uttered. Bonnie sat quietly beside her Granny, she abruptly replied, "we lived in Granny's car for a long time." I turned to Mrs. Green, "you mean you and bonnie have been living in your car?" Bonnie uttered, "ugh...ugh...yeah...right, Granny." We didn't have a place to stay." Mrs. Green dropped her head in shame...looking for words to explain. She blabbered, "well, after my husband died, a couple months later, Bonnie's mother was killed in a drug bust in California. The rent got so far behind. No matter how hard I tried to catch up on the payments, the landlord just wanted me out." She wiped her eyes. I don't know why I am here. It's just seem like I was drawn this way by a force that I can't explain." Bonnie replied, "it took us a long time to get here." Mrs. Green folded her arms, "yes, we made it. We had no where else to go. Many doors have been closed in our face."

We talked for several more minutes. Unexpectedly, my heart felt compassion for her and Bonnie. I asked, "Mrs. Green, how would you and Bonnie like to live here with me and my family?" Mrs. Green twisted her head around quickly. She answered, "oh, can we, Mrs. Maggie. Do you really mean it? Live with you. Oh, God bless you." She blabbered, "thank you, thank you." Tears began to stream down her cheeks. Bonnie wiped her grandmother eyes with happiness in her voice. She shrugged, "don't cry Grandma." Mrs. Carter will help us now." Mrs. Green cried, I don't want to be a burden. I can work for our stay here with you." Bonnie beamed with excitement, "I can help, too. I was overjoyed with the idea. I responded, "okay. My housekeeper needs to retire due to her back problems if I can find someone to take her place.

Mrs. France has been working for me since Sanato first came home from the hospital. She was the first to share the secret of my son's ability to see. Her back gives out all the time. The doctor asked her to stop working two years ago. Mrs. Green replied, "well, I am ready to work. Just say when." I will notify Mrs. France tomorrow. I think we have done enough gossiping to last for a long time." Mrs. Green hesitated, "my, this is a big place. I am going to love working for you Mrs. Maggie." Not knowing any other way to express her gratitude, she bounced up from her chair, "ugh...I...can start right now, Mrs. Maggie. Just show me where to begin."

I had never seen anyone so excited. I didn't try to stop her. She looked curiously around the rooms. She reacted like a child on his visit to a circus. She wandered back through the door and beamed, "this house is very large. Someone like me could get lost for days." I suggested that we bring her things inside. She had all of her possessions in the car. I helped them move into the guesthouse. Mrs. Green sighed with relief. "I don't know why I brought all my things

with me today. It just seemed like the right thing to do."
Bonnie clinged to her Grandma's arm. She begged, "come on
let's go see the house, Granny." She rushed towards the
house and left her bags on the ground. I shouted, "the door is
unlocked."

Sanato and Tim arrived home about the same time. I
introduced Mrs. Green to the rest of my family. Tim and
Sanato were very polite. Tim remembered Mrs. Green and her
little girl. Sanato went to his room. Suddenly, Bonnie busted
in the door screaming, "Grandma, Grandma, that old man
with the blanket is here." Mrs. Green tried to calm Bonnie
down. She replied, "I'm sure it was just your imagination.
That old man is not here." Mrs. Green placed her arms
around Bonnie. She glanced around with a veil of happiness
covering her face. Tim and I smiled...for we understood the
mystery of the old man. When Bonnie eyes fell upon Sanato'
s face, she forgot all about the old man. Bonnie made her
way over to Sanato's chair. Her eyes fixed upon his face. I
responded, "Bonnie, this is my son Sanato and my husband
Tim." She glanced at Tim briefly. She answered, "hi," and
quickly directed her attention to Sanato. She blabbed, "hi, my
name is Bonnie. I love all your shades and things." Sanato
answered, "well, hi...I see you have already checked out my
room. Which pair do you like the best?" Bonnie eyes
widened. She replied, "I like the silver and black pair."
Sanato nodded his head, "that's my favorite pair, too." She
looked down, wanting Sanato to believe in her. She uttered,
"I did see that old man. He was the same old man that helped
me to walk." Sanato sputtered a quick apology. "I believe

you, Bonnie. I have seen that old man, too." " How can he be in two places at the same time? We saw him back home?" Mrs. Green listened quietly. Sanato uttered with pride, "you see, that old man is everywhere. He's just like the wind blowing among the trees." Bonnie began to laugh at Sanato's silly notion. Before long, everyone was laughing together.

Sanato didn't ask any questions about Mrs. Green and her granddaughter. He was sure they were someone we had known in the past. Mrs. Green and Bonnie put their things away. I prepared dinner. As we sit down to eat, Bonnie demanded, "may I sit besides Sanato?" I nodded, "sure you can, here take my chair." Bonnie didn't hesitate to move her long legs with an inquisitive look in her eyes. She boasted, "do you wear your glasses all the time?" Sanato grinned, "no...only when I am eating." Bonnie glanced at me; "no...do you sleep in those things?" Mrs. Green retorted, "Bonnie, will you please stop asking so many question? Don't you see Sanato is trying to eat?" Sanato shrugged, "why don't I end the suspense." He reached for his glasses. I quickly shouted, "no Son, not now. Please lets just wait awhile longer." Mrs. Green nodded her head...thanking me for not allowing Sanato to take off his glasses. Tim rubbed his stomach after stuffing down three pieces of chicken. He beamed, "Honey, dinner was wonderful. That fried chicken was the best." Mrs. Green began removing the dirty dishes from the table. She insisted, "I will clear off the table."

Sanato and Bonnie continued to sit at the table. I could hear her asking Sanato more questions. Finally, he asked, "Bonnie, what grade are you in?" Her smile faded away. Holding her head down slightly, she glanced up at him. She quickly looked at her grandmother for comfort. Mrs. Green frowned, "Bonnie, what's wrong?" Her delicate jaws tightened with a tremble in her voice and she stuttered, "well, I ...ugh I should have been in the ninth grade. Because I was sick all the time, Grandmother said I had to stay at home." Sanato reacted, "your legs, they are fine now?" She took a big swallow of milk, "yeah, it was very strange. You know that old man I was telling you about, well, he told me to drink plenty of milk and my legs would grow stronger." Sanato loved to hear things about the old man. Because he knew that old man was truly his great grandfather. He requested, "tell me more about that old man. Was he carrying a blanket?" Mrs. Green exclaimed, "yes...yes he was. The blanket was old and worn out." Sanato remarked with a touch of intrigue in his voice, "ugh...ugh...yeah. Sounds like the blanket is the mystery behind this old fellow." Bonnie moved her food around on her plate. She declared, "look like he was lost or he didn't have any friends."

I smiled and thought to myself, well, thank you again Grandpa, you helped me out on this one. Sanato shrugged, Mom, what are you beaming about?" Bonnie and her grandmother waited for my answer. I responded, "oh, I was just thanking God and someone else for all the good things that have come our way." Sanato pushed his chin out, "for a wonderful son like me?" I planted a kiss on Sanato's forehead. Mrs. Green replied, Mrs. Maggie, you have a wonderful family. I thank you for everything you have done for Bonnie and me. Having a roof over our heads and food for my little girl is a blessing. Now you don't have to worry about paying me... just allowing me to work is fine." I was hoping not to offend her, I stated, "now stop that. I am going to pay you for every minute you work for me." Tim eyed me with studious attention...giving me a presumptuous grin. He boasted, "you see my wife is one of the kind. When God made her, he threw away the mold. I love her very much." My eyes filled with tears. I remembered the words of my grandparents. They taught me to show compassion for someone less fortunate than self. Warmth filled my heart for these wonderful people surrounding my life. I blabbered, "now stop all this talking about me. How about some desert?" Bonnie yelled, "yeah, its banana pudding time." Sanato asked, "how did you know we were having banana pudding for desert?" Bonnie flashed a big smile. Obviously proud of the fact that she stirred the pudding mix. She teased, "because I helped to make the desert."

Mrs. Green and Bonnie became family to us. Bonnie was the daughter I always wanted. The first time I laid eyes on her, I knew there were something distinctive about her frail little body. Even though, I tried with all my will to make her walk, strangely as it was, nothing happened. Yet, here she sits before me. The wonders supplied by my grandfather's spirit presided over the destiny of others. The house became a haven of love with everyone giving of himself or herself. Bonnie and Sanato became the best of friends. One day Sanato took off his eye cover and showed her his face. Bonnie face lit up with amazement, gesture, yet, she was not alarmed. She touched Sanato's face with her fingertips and smiled, "you are different. Its because God made you that way. One day he will give you eyes. Just like he made me walk."

When they went out together, Bonnie would wear one of Sanato's old eye covers. Tim and I reacted without Sanato's knowledge. He was born with endowed power to see...with a transcendent ability beyond human comprehension. His behavior was impressive for someone so young. We baffled the attempt to explain the mystery. Sanato's thick brows knitted upon his forehead. Implausible layers of skin replaced his eyes. Mrs. Green and Bonnie loved my son for his inner character, not for his appearance. They were curious about what Sanato concealed under his peculiar glasses. After he showed his face to them the first time, nothing else was ever discussed about my son. Mrs. Green worked hard to keep the house clean. Sanato found time to tutor Bonnie after school. Bonnie's grades improved and her teacher moved her up to another grade level. Bonnie was two years older that Sanato, but two grades behind in school. She was a part of this family. We treated her as a daughter. One day Tim and Bonnie returned from the store and she was very upset. I reached out for her with opened arms, "Bonnie, what's wrong?" She cried, "I saw some of my classmates at the store and they teased me." Tim said, "they were joking with her. One of the girls asked Bonnie if I was her father. Before Bonnie responded to their question, the girl shouted out, "yes, that's her daddy, he's black." Bonnie wiped her eyes, "why do some people slander other people's name. I don't understand?" Sanato paused, "the word for that is racism." "No…I declared, inhuman is the word for people that impose discrimination against other races." I began to tell them about the time I was faced with bias. Bonnie's mood changed. As I conversed about my life growing upon the farm. Sanato asked, "Mama, did that really happen to you?" Tim smiled, showing me how proud he was. Knowing it took courage and a loving heart to endure.

Sanato asked, "Bonnie, do you want to go for a ride?" Bonnie answered with an excited pitch in her voice. "Yeah…I am wearing the red and white eye cover." "Okay, he uttered, the silver and black one for me." They plunged out the door…leaving echoes of laughter trailing behind them. Tim gazed at me shaking his head. "Today has been one of those days you don't want to remember." I replied, "yes, I know I heard talk around town, too. The blacks discriminated against us. Tim asked, "what have we done?" I nodded, "certain Black families are not pleased with the fact that we invited a white woman and her granddaughter into our home. We gave the white lady a job when there are many black families who need to work." Tim expressed disappointment, "well…that clarifies why Mr. Davison didn't speak to me this morning. I have observed some changes in some of the people at church , too. They don't call me anymore and smiles are very few." One Sunday after church, we discovered our car with a slashed tire. We didn't want to believe someone from the church was responsible…especially the black people that we have known for so long. In spite of everything that happens to us, we didn't make any change in our decisions.

We continued to serve the Lord. Mrs. Green and Bonnie went to church every Sunday. One Sunday the minister preached a sermon about the Good Samaritan. The minister's words were appropriate for our hearts were heavy. Tears began to slowly flow down my cheeks. Before long everyone was crying. Several of the members walked up to the prayer bench, with their heads down asking forgiveness for their sins. After services no one said a word. There was lots of hugging and kissing among the members. From that day forward, we were all treated with love and respect. The congregation was spiritually regenerated. Mrs. Green became the first white Assistant Sunday school teacher. She was a gentle woman...ready to shower anyone with love. All of the kids loved her. The church people began to smile and encourage love among them. We donated a large amount of money towards the building fund. Tim took the youth on church trips twice a year.

Time passed so quickly. Sanato and Bonnie filled the house with joy. Bonnie was a junior in high school and Sanato will graduate this summer. He goes out quite often with his special friend, Gail. Sometimes I notice her staring at Bonnie with envious eyes. Sanato informed me that Gail had asked him why he spends so much time with her. Even though Bonnie had lots of friends, she liked to spend most of her time with Sanato. He treated her like a sister...never allowing her to feel left out. Gail surely didn't approve of this, but she kept quite when Bonnie was present. Sanato gave Gail a birthday party. I thought everything was fine until I heard Bonnie soft voice at my door. She cried, "Mrs. Carter, can I talk with you?" "Yes, what's wrong? Why are you crying?" She nodded her head and wiped her tears from her eyes. "Mrs. Carter, my feelings for Sanato are very special. I know he think of me as a sister. I am afraid I have fallen in love with him." I nodded my head in amazement. "Why Bonnie, I am sorry. I know my son cares for you. Have you talked to Sanato about your feelings?" Bonnie continued to twist her fingers together in an unsetting manner. She murmured, "no...I feel so happy when I am with him. I can't stand for him to spend so much time with Gail. He is my friend, too." I listened but not sure I knew the answer for her. Yet, I understood her. She had fallen in love with Sanato. He was not aware of the transformation of their relationship. I didn't know what advice to give Bonnie. Nothing I said that night made any difference with her. Bonnie was madly in love with my son. He respected her as a sister.

Weeks passed and Bonnie became withdrawn from everyone. Mrs. Green didn't know why she stayed in her room all the time. Finally, one day she asked me. I related the night Bonnie came to me crying. Mrs. Green reacted, "oh no. Why did this have to happen? They were like a sister and a brother. I guess things change and feelings get in the way. She will be okay, I will have a talk with her." Bonnie began hanging out with new friends. She avoided Sanato and Gail. We didn't tell Sanato the reason Bonnie spent most of her time in her room.

One morning Mrs. Green told me Bonnie had decided to move out. I was shocked at the idea of her moving in with someone else. Mrs. Green insisted that she wanted Bonnie to be happy. I nodded my head in a teary eyed agreement. I knew the real reason she wanted to move because of Sanato's relationship with Gail. Mrs. Green asked, "what else can we do? We can't tell Sanato the real reason she is moving out." I thought, there's no need to tell him. There is nothing he can do. It will only make things difficult for him. Bonnie passed the door as we were discussing her problem. I shouted, "Bonnie, can we talk with you." She slowly turned towards us with an expression on her face ...don't lecture me attitude. I replied, "Bonnie, I wish we could persuade you to stay. But, looks like your mind is already made up." Bonnie nodded her head while not looking at her Grandmother or me. She was acting if she was about to breakdown and cry. She uttered, "I will be fine. My friends will help me." Mrs. Green replied, "baby, if you ever need anything, just call me. I have something to help you get settled in." She pulled out a brown envelope from her purse. Bonnie took the envelope and her smile faded as she glanced around towards me. She quickly looked away from the questions in my eyes. I reached out for her, embracing her as my own while fighting back tears. I uttered, "I'm going to miss you. Take care of yourself and don't hesitate to call us for anything."

Sanato and Gail entered the room as Bonnie was leaving. Sanato blabbered in a rapid tone, "what's going on...are we interrupting something?" Mrs. Green answered, "hi Sanato, Bonnie is moving in with some of her friends for a while." Sanato asked, "why is she moving out? Is everything okay?" Gail waited eagerly for an answer. "Everything is fine, I replied. This was Bonnie's decision to move out." Gail uttered in a serenity tone; "Sanato and Bonnie were very close. I know he will miss her." Sanato paced the floor, "well, it's not like she's leaving the country...right? Hey, what's cooking...I'm starving." Mrs. Green exclaimed, "fried steak with gravy and creamed potatoes."

Bonnie flounced in carrying her suitcase. She gave Gail a quick emotional stare. She then uttered, "Granny, will you take me to my friend's house? It's only a few miles from here." Sanato replied, "so you're moving out. Hey, we are going to miss you." Bonnie's lips trembled. "I will miss all of you, too. I forgot tot tell everyone. I also have a job." Mrs. Green blabbered out in surprise, "a job why that's great. We just want the best for you." I watched Gail as she inched her way towards Sanato. She had a pleasing expression on her face. Neither one of them knew the real reason Bonnie was moving out. She put her arms around Sanato...making Bonnie feel even more miserable. Gail beamed in a jolly tone, "of course, we will miss you. I hope you enjoy your job." Gail showed signs of hypocrisy. She was happy that Bonnie was moving out. Bonnie glanced away from my eyes. Fighting back the tears with confidence in her tone of voice, she laughingly said, "I am going to be fine." Making her way to the door she glanced back and said, "I will miss all of you...especially you Sanato. Giving him a hug and clinging on to his arm, Gail quickly spoke up, "oh Bonnie, please stay in touch with me." Sanato carried Bonnie's suitcase to the car, leaving Gail standing alone. Mrs. Green took the day off to help Bonnie move into her new place. We waved as she drove off...leaving us standing on lawn. Sanato uttered, "I can't understand why Bonnie wants to move away. I treated her like the sister I never had." I retorted, "she will be back. I hope she will come to her senses soon." Gail interrupted with an insensitive remark about Bonnie, "well, have you all forgotten I am here? There's no need to feel sorry for Bonnie. She has done just what she wanted to do, move out." I simply turned towards Gail with a negative look in my eyes. "Oh, Gail don't get your feathers bent out of shape. We know you are here." Sanato asked, "girl...you are not jealous, are you?" He kissed her softly. Reassuring her that she was tops on his list. Gail gave me a sour look and uttered, "Sanato are we going to the movies tonight?" Sanato moved in my direction, "oh yes Mama, we are going to a movie. Is there anything I can do for you before we go?" I replied, "no, I will be fine. Go ahead and have a good time." Sanato and Gail drove off.

◆

CHAPTER 20

"THE DISAPPOINTMENT"

The phone rang and I was hoping it would be Tim. I hurried back into the house. The voice on the other end didn't sound like some one I knew. A male voice startled me. He asked, "may I speak with the parent of Sanato Carter." I took a deep breath, "yes, I am Mrs. Carter." He replied, "Mrs. Carter this is Mr. Carl Braxton. Do you have a minute?" Not knowing what he wanted, I quickly responded, "Yes, I do." The voice on the other end declared, "I work for the University of Maryland. I have some great news for your son." I blabbered, "yes, yes, what kind of news?" He continued, "we are calling concerning your son's future education." I listened carefully, pressing the phone closer to my ear. Mr. Braxton continued, "you see, Mrs. Carter, the company that supplied your son's eye cover is a branch from our firm. He asked, "your son graduates this year? Am I correct?" "Yes he does, I beamed, waiting for him to continue. He uttered in a husky tone; "here's the good news. We are offering your son a four-year scholarship. Now isn't that wonderful?" "What," I shouted. You are giving him a scholarship?" He replied, "we have received your son's grades for the last three years. The school provides all the information we need. We are looking for students with outstanding grade average." I pressed the phone closer to my ear...not wanting to miss a word he was saying. He continued, "Mrs. Carter I know this is a great surprise for you. I hope you will discuss this with your son. This is a great opportunity." "Yes, this is a surprise," I acknowledged. "You will receive a letter from us within a few weeks. Thank you for your time. I am looking forward to meeting you and your family. Have a good day." I gripped the phone to my ear. They wanted to give my son a scholarship to the University of Maryland. The school was well known for their Research and Development laboratories.

Angry rages flashed through my mind. The Biaglass Company assured us that Sanato files would be confidential. They had sent his records to a research school without our permission. The doctors questioned us about our son. We refused the research test. I recognized the mystery of my son. He was born into a world filled with interrogation. The doctors are not aware of Sanato's ability to see without eyes. Tim and I knew that our son's secret would not stay hidden forever. I discussed the phone call with Tim. He was very agitated with the Biaglass company. They promised Sanato's condition would be confidential.

As time passed, we waited for words from Mr. Braxton. After several months passed, we called the school. No one knew anything about a scholarship for my son. We questioned them over and over again. They gave us the same answer. Mr. Braxton was not a part of the university. I wondered why he lied to us. I am sure he had a lot to gain. Research labs are always looking for someone or something to use as a Guinea Pig. I am sure my son's secret had been exposed without our knowledge.

Tim and I decided to inform Sanato about Mr. Braxton's call. He reacted in a positive manner. "Well, you can't blame him for trying. I am a very unique human being." He continued, "I'm surprise we have not been on the front page of the newspaper." Tim responded, "we knew the day would come to this. I am thankful you are old enough to handle people like Mr. Braxton." "Why didn't they tell us that our son's records had been sent to the research lab," I asked. "You know there are other people behind this. Maybe, the hospital where Sanato was born was involved. Mr. Braxton was just the message carrier. I am sure he will call on us again." "You know I never did trust the company that made Sanato' s glasses," I responded. They sure did try to separate us in the examination room." Sanato uttered, "yeah, I was scared to move from your side. Everytime they touched me, I wanted to say, I can see you."

A knock on the door interrupted our conversation. Sanato answered the door. Gail busted in thrilled by Sanato's charming smile. She blabbered, "Sanato let's go to the mall...or do you have other plans." He planted a kiss on her cheek, eyeing me. She beamed, "hi, Mr. And Mrs. Carter." Sanato answered "no, I don't have any plans. I am at your disposal." Gail took charge of the relationship. She arranged every weekend for shopping. Everytime the door opened or the phone rang, it would be Gail. Each time her finger sparkled with a new ring or her wrist had a diamond bracelet dingling loosely for my eyes to behold. Sometimes I would ask her about her lovely jewelry. She would always answer, "your son has good taste." Whenever Gail came around, I just resented her presence.

I missed Bonnie. She didn't call or visit unless she needed money. I worried about her. She wasn't the same girl I had known in the past. Bonnie would always be in a hurry to leave, even when Sanato was home. I asked her about her job one day. She duly uttered, "I work the night shift." Bonnie borrowed money and stole from us, too. I began to miss money from my purse. Shortly after her brief visits. Even Mrs. Green was aware of the changes. One day we stopped by to visit Bonnie. No one answered the door. We could hear them laughing inside. Mrs. Green worried a lot about Bonnie. She would never open up to her Grandmother. She gave us the impression that she didn't want us to interfere with her life.

Several weeks passed with no word from Mr. Braxton. So, we put the matter aside. However, one day Mr. Braxton did call and we agreed to see him. I was sure he would be able to answer our questions. The meeting with Mr. Braxton was not what we expected. He greeted us with a big smile, a camera, and a notebook pad in his hand. Sanato paced nervously across the floor. Mr. Braxton uttered, "so you are the mystery boy I have heard so much about. Sanato shied away from him. Suddenly, he pulled the camera out and began to snap pictures of Sanato. Tim knocked the camera on the floor. Mr. Braxton picked up the camera and said, "what the hell are you doing?" Tim lurked forwardly, "we didn't give you permission to take pictures of our son." Mr. Braxton stumbled back frantically. His mouth fell open. He exclaimed, "I'm going to need pictures before I can allow you to sign these scholarship papers, while shaking a hand full of forms. I sensed the anger building up in Sanato. I squealed, "Mr. Braxton, I think you better leave now." Mr. Braxton scrutinized me with determination. "You don't understand...ugh...there is plenty of money to be made...yeah...ugh...all I need is one picture, just one." Tim face contorted with anger and he shouted, "scoundrel, you would sell your own mother for a profit." Mr. Braxton's remarks antagonized Tim and as he lurched forward, he yelled to Mr. Braxton to "get out now." Suddenly Mr. Braxton' s camera dropped to the floor again. Each time he reached down to pick up the camera, it would move away. He tried to grab it. He looked up at Sanato..."well, I be damned. Did you see that...my camera moving...ugh...I...what's going on here?" He stammered, tumbling against the wall. Everything occurred very fast. Sanato had this weird expression on his face. "No, Sanato, don't hurt him," I screamed.

Mr. Braxton stumbled out of the door and Tim slammed it behind him. We waited for the car to drive away. After a few minutes, Tim peeped out of the window..."wait a minute, there's another man in the car with him. Where did he come from?" Mr. Braxton's head rested against the seat with an awkward expression on his face. His eyes rolled back in a bewildered spell and the car speeded away with a cloud of dust. Sanato asked, "who was that driving the car?" Your great grandfather, I thought. Tim uttered, "that's strange, he came out here by himself." I felt my grandfather's presence in the house, I uttered. Sanato grinned with a stunned look on his face, "yeah, so did I. Mr. Braxton won't remember anything about this visit. I am sure my great grandfather will drive him safely home." "Where ever home might be."

We never heard from Mr. Braxton again. However, one night as we watched the late news, Sanato frantically yelled, "look...look there's Mr. Braxton on the news." "Yeah, that's him all right." Sure enough there he was wearing a bright yellow rain coat...assisting the thousand of people surrounding him. I beamed with delight, thinking to myself...um...um, Grandpa you are a saint. I was even more surprised when the news stated the name of the place, Gambia, Africa. Tim boasted with excitement. "Wow," now he has a lot to keep him busy." Sanato scratched his head in amazement. He uttered, "I wonder how he got there," with a silly grin on his face. We never heard anything from Mr. Braxton again. We knew his lengthy trip had a mysterious touch.

Late one evening the phone rung and I heard Bonnie's voice on the other end. "Mrs. Carter, I'm in big trouble, please let me speak to my grandmother." I knew something was wrong from the tone of Bonnie's voice. "Okay Bonnie," I replied. "Calm down, I will get her." Mrs. Green was cleaning the kitchen, but after she heard Bonnie's name, she hurried to the phone. Almost out of breath, she asked, "what...what's...ugh wrong, Bonnie?" Mrs. Green turned to me with a disturbed look in her eyes. "Bonnie is in jail." "What happened," I asked? Mrs. Green pleaded with Bonnie to stop crying. "I am on my way." She grabbed her purse from the table, tears in her eyes, she uttered in an emotional

tone, "and the policemen found drugs in Bonnie's purse."
Tim demanded, "we will go with you."

When we arrived, the officer explained that Bonnie
and her friends have been under surveillance for several
months. During the house search, drugs were found in her
possession. Mrs. Green nervously asked, "may I see my
child?" The officer insisted, "will you please have a seat?"
There are forms to be filled out before Bonnie can be released
on bond." "Bond," Mrs. Green blurted out. How much is her
bond?" The officer pulled a brown folder from his file cabinet.
He pushed his glasses up on his narrow nose. He replied,
"her bond is $2,000." Mrs. Green fumbled with the zipper of
her purse. She frantically murmured, "I don't have that much
money." The officer answered, "Mrs., you only pay a
percentage of that amount which will cost you $200." Mrs.
Green eyes filled with tears as she passed the officer the
money. Upon inspecting the money, he stated, "Mrs. Green, I'
m sorry this is not enough money. I need $125 more dollars."
That was all the money she had. Tim immediately wrote a
check for the balance.

We waited for another hour. Suddenly, the door
opened and Bonnie ran to her Grandmother in the midst of all
the sobbing. The officer replied, "Miss Green, I am going to
warn you. Please don't leave the state. Your court day is two
weeks from today." I watched Bonnie with sympathetic eyes.
He continued, "please for your sake, be on time." Her
appearance had completely changed. She wore gaudy
clothes, which made her appear older. Her skin was
tarnished from wearing inexpensive make-up. Her short bob

cut contoured her narrow face. A noticeable tattoo was silhouette on her arm. Tim asked, "Bonnie are you okay? Did they hassle you?" "No, she uttered, I just hate jail cells." Mrs. Green embraced Bonnie. "Come on, I am taking you home with me," she insisted. She inspected her with curious eyes. "Why did you cut your hair so short," Mrs. Green asked? Bonnie just hunched her shoulders and said, "I couldn't do anything with my hair, so I cut it off." Tim grinned, "I think she looks like Demi Moore.

We stopped by to pick up Bonnie's things. The place was a mess; clothes were all over the floor. Dirty dishes were stacked high in the sink and a sickening odor overpowered us at the door. Three other girls were there. They looked like tramps. Tattoos spotted their small frame bodies making them appear even more bizarre. We stood outside the door while Bonnie gathered up her things. Mrs. Green asked, "do all of these girls live here?" Bonnie uttered, "no, they live across the street." The oldest girl blabbered in a firm tone; "our sister lives here. We hang out over here all the time." She looked around and said, "Bonnie, we are going to miss you, Girl. You can always come back when you get ready."

Tim took Bonnie's suitcase to the car. As we walked away, two men passed us. One of them grinned. "Hey...ugh...yeah...Bonnie, see you got out the joint rather quick. Yeah...ugh...we see you tonight, right?" he signaled there were drugs in his possession by patting his back pocket. Bonnie gave him a silly grin while she walked away with her head down. Mrs. Green sadly acknowledged in a reluctant voice, "I thought you had better judgement about people."

Bonnie answered in a defensive tone, "Grandmother, they are nice people. They are not rich like...Mr. and Mrs. Carter, but they are my friends." Mrs. Green nodded her head in disbelief. She requested, "I don't want you hanging around them anymore." Bonnie stammered, but...Grandmother...I ...ugh...I ugh." "I don't want you over there," Mrs. Green yelled. "I made a mistake when I allowed you to move out." Mrs. Green expressed sadness. Bonnie sat silent, tears forming in her eyes. Tim glanced at me. "I suggested we all sleep on the subject."

Sanato returned home after his date with Gail. We informed him about Bonnie's problem. He didn't want to believe that Bonnie was implicated with drugs. Tim and Sanato strolled off to the kitchen. I relaxed on the sofa and kicked off my shoes. My thoughts were whirling around in my head. I closed my eyes for a second. I could hear Sanato and his father discussing what had happened tonight with Bonnie.

Suddenly, Mrs. Green's voice shattered my thoughts with her screams that echoed with a desperate pitch. I opened the door and she fell in screaming..."call 911...Bonnie has shot herself." Tim and Sanato dashed from the kitchen and Tim dialed the emergency number. Sanato bounced ahead, racing full speed out of the door. The sight of Bonnie lying across her bed froze me in my tracks. Bonnie's blood was splattered all over the wall. The gun lay besides her limp body. Mrs. Green screamed, "oh no, God no." Sanato cradled Bonnie in his arms while rocking her like a baby. He called her name over and over again. Mrs. Green collapsed on the floor. Tim helped her up into a chair. I embraced Sanato. "Son, she's dead. You can't help her now." He continued to rock Bonnie. Tim pulled Sanato away because the paramedics had arrived. We looked on while in a state of shock, while they frantically tried to revive her. The coroner pronounced her dead. The paramedic placed her body inside the ambulance.

Sanato cried out, "why did this have to happen to her? She was so full of life." A bloodstained note lay on the bed. Mrs. Green screamed, "oh God, my baby is dead, why...why." Tim's eyes betrayed his sadness as he reached for my hand. I picked up the note and it read: Dear Grandmother, first of all I want to say, "I love you." You have been the best friend I could ever ask for. I am sorry that drugs have directed me down the wrong pathway. I have been living a lie from the day I moved out. It's easier to write about my pain instead of literally to you. Drugs destroyed my sense of reason, my value and my heart. Dying is the only way to relieve the pain of living...signed Bonnie. I passed the note to Mrs. Green. She grasped the letter tightly. "No, no, she screamed in a loud grieved tone. "Why did she kill herself? I loved her no matter what she did." We tried to console Mrs. Green. Sanato sit motionless on the bed.

Tim insisted that Mrs. Green stay with us. We spent the night calling relatives for her. We discussed Bonnie's funeral arrangement. The police ruled it as a suicide. Mrs. Green had no insurance, so we arranged for Bonnie to be buried next to my grandparents. The service was set for the following Sunday. The church was packed with visitors and friends. A crowd had to wait outside the church door. Most of Bonnie's friends were there. All of them sat nervously in the back of the church. Sanato and Gail sat beside us. She held on to his hand. The church members mourned the loss of Bonnie. As they lowed her coffin into the ground, my heart skipped frantically in my chest. I remembered her as a little girl in her wheelchair. Now she lay besides the people I cared for so much. Tears soaked my face, as I had these thoughts. Bonnie is dead. Tim gripped my hand and we walked to the car. Several families followed us home. There was plenty of food because the church members had helped us dearly.

Bonnie's death was a tragic loss. It reminded me of the death of my best friend, Kim. I was only fourteen years old at that time. Months after the funeral, rumors spread around town about Bonnie. They said, she worked as a call girl...dealing powerfully in the drug ring. One of her friends stated that Bonnie was pregnant when she died. We didn't want to believe the town gossip. Several days later Mrs. Green was gathered Bonnie's things up for the Salvation Army. As she unpacked the suitcase, she found two large bags of drugs concealed inside the lining. We knew the truth had been revealed about Bonnie's life.

Sanato and Gail announced their engagement several months after Bonnie's death. He spent most of his time with Gail. We saw less and less of him each day. Even though the relationship seemed perfect from the outer surface, I still had doubts about Gail. I held as aversion against her, which I only felt. My son gave her an expensive diamond ring for her birthday. Gail loved the lavish gifts he was able to buy her.

Sometimes I wonder if he had been just a ordinary fellow, would she had dated him. Sanato had his won savings and checking accounts. I didn't realize how much money he was spending on her gifts until I began checking his bank statements. I was totally amazed at the amount of money he had spent. I took it upon myself to have a long talk with my son on this issue. After my conversation with him, Gail visits became less frequent. She only stayed a short time when she stopped by. Sanato's spirit began to change. Stress related actions were affecting their relationship. Sanato's erratic behavior showed signs of depression. One Saturday night he returned home early, and I asked, why was he home so early? He nodded shyly, "Gail wanted to use the car so she dropped me off." I gestured nervously at the idea, "where's her car?" He replied, "her parents are going out of town. You know they only have one car. I didn't see any reason not to let her use my car." "Where did she go." I demanded. Sanato paced nervously across the floor. "She invited some of her friends to a Sorority meeting."

We passed the time by chatting about the crossroads of life. After about three hours, Sanato began to show signs of anxiety. "Are you okay," I asked? After realizing I wasn't lecturing him or trying to interfere in his affairs, Sanato slumped down in a chair. Finally he murmured, "Mama, you think Gail is using me for my money, don't you?" I paused for a second, hoping for the right words. "Son, you can never be certain about anything in this life, except death. You sure can't put a price tag on love. To love and be loved is to feel the sun from both sides. Take things a little slower. Watch for signs of disappointment in her face when you stop buying her gifts." Sanato listened attentively. He checked the time again. "You are right, Mama." He stammered, "I am going to look for her."

The click of Tim's keys in the door disrupted my thoughts. "Hey, what's wrong," he uttered as he kissed me lightly. Sanato replied, "Daddy, I let Gail use my car. It's been a long time and she hasn't called me. I am worried about her." Tim glanced at me. My voice showed signs of doubts as I said, "why won't she call him?" Sanato stepped towards the door, "well, I am tired of waiting. Mama, may I borrow your car?" Pleased by the prospect of finding Gail, I swiftly passed him my keys. Sanato rushed out the door. Tim assured me that he would probably find Gail and her friends having a good time.

♦

CHAPTER 21
"THE PHENONENON CHANGES"

We waited for Sanato to return. After about two hours or more, hysterics took it toil. We scoured the streets for hours looking for Sanato. Tim suggested that we go back to the house in case he had already returned. As we approached our house, we noticed two police cars parked in our driveway. My heart stops beating for a second. "Oh God, oh God, something has happened, I know it." We rushed toward the police car and Tim yelled, "officers...is anything wrong?" The policeman asked, "are you the parents of Sanato Karen Carter?" My legs weakened as I clinged to Tim's arm. My heart stopped beating for a moment. "Yes, yes, we are Sanato's parents?" The policeman exclaimed, "there's been an tragic accident. Please come with us, we will drive you to the hospital." I closed my eyes and prayed, "oh God, please let my son be okay."

The message from my grandfather flashed through my mind, "a life began, a life will end." Tim cradled me tightly and without a word we merged together praying for the safety of our son. The hospital where the policemen took us was only about ten minutes away. We went straight to the emergency room. Tim and I dashed through the automatic doors. Several of the doctors acknowledged us as we entered. "Are you the parents of Sanato Carter?" The senior doctor spoke in a husky voice, "please come with me." I gripped Tim for support. My legs weaken with each step and the nurse assisted me. All I could think about was my son. I took a deep breath and uttered, "where's my son?" The nurse directed us to another room down the hall. From a distance I noticed my son lying on the table with a sheet draped over his body. I screamed, "no, not my baby, no...no." The doctor stated, "Mrs. Carter, your son never realized what happened. He died instantly."

Tim helped me over to the table. My hands trembled as I reached out to touch the sheet. "Sanato, oh my son," I shouted in pain. Tim lifted the sheet from Sanato's body. Tears blinded my sight. I dried my eyes to focus. When I gazed upon my son's face, no words could explain what my eyes beheld. My son had eyes. They were open and staring directly at us. The doctor replied, "we tried to close his eyes, but for some strange reason, they wouldn't close. We are going to leave you and your husband alone with your son."

I reached out to touch Sanato's hand. The feeling of warmth rushed through my fingertips. Tim's eyes betrayed the hurt in his heart as he stared down at his son. I leaned against Sanato's body. Something very strange happened, my muscles suddenly became rigid. My face flushed with sweat. I screamed, "oh my God, my son is not dead...oh no, he is not dead...Tim...Tim...look." Tim's eyes widened as he turned to face me. He grabbed me while making a murmuring sound, "ugh...Mag...Mag...ugh...my God, what's happened to your face? You...you...ugh...look...so different. Your face...ugh...your...hair...you." He grabbed my hands. Something astounding has occurred."

I glared at Tim. "Your face...you have changed too, Tim. Your hair, it is not gray anymore." I gripped Sanato's hand tighter. The warmth gradually vanished. The room became still. Suddenly, the blanket appeared as a cloud overshadowing Sanato's body, and with a perennial smile on his face, his eyes slowly closed. Tim cried, "no, no, help him please. Don't take him away from us. He can't be dead. Sanato, Sanato?" There were neither bloodstains nor cuts anywhere on his body. His neck had been broken which killed him instantly. One of his little fingers hung loose from his hand. We kissed him good-by.

Before he left this world, he gave us back our youth. Our lives were transformed within seconds. The doctors returned and they stared at us with inquisitive looks on their faces. Tim and I gazed at each other. He put his arms around me. We accepted the fact that we would never see our son again. The doctors were still in questioning, not sure if we were the same people. One of the doctors touched me on the shoulder and uttered, "Yes...are you Mrs. Carter? It's time to take your son's body." His eyes never moved from our faces as he gazed attentively. They rolled Sanato's body towards the door. I noticed his shoes sticking from under the sheet. I cried, "stop...stop...pleas give me my son's shoes." The doctor pulled off the shoes and placed them in my hand. I squeezed them close to my chest. Two other doctors came in just as they pushed the body down the hallway. One of the doctors asked, "where are the parents of Sanato Carter?" Tim answered in a meek tone; "we are his parents." The doctor gave us a second glance. "We are sorry about your son. May God be with you. Would you like to go to the chapel? There is one down the hallway to your right." As we walked away, the doctors whispered, "they seem so young to have a son that old...there's some peculiar about those two. I saw them when they came in earlier and they didn't appear that young." I held on tightly to Sanato's shoes. His spirit will be with me forever. Maybe, he will return to this world, not as our son, but as a star in heaven...or maybe a cloud floating above.

We shared life with our son for eighteen years. He was a mystery from the day he was conceived in my womb. His birth and death hold a great mystery, which will never be revealed. He was given the gift of life, which he gave back to us. Maybe, Sanato had one wish before he died. He wished that he had eyes, I thought. Tim and I stopped by the office and signed the death release form. I held my son shoes closer to my side. The nurse looked at us strangely. She asked, "would you like for me to put those shoes in a bag? I am sorry about your son." I softly uttered, no, I want to hold them in my hand." The nurse pushed her glasses upon her nose and began typing . She asked again, "are you Sanato's biological parents?" We nodded, "yes we are." She stammered, "well...ugh...you both look so very young. You don't look old enough to be Sanato's parents." Tim and I smiled, for we knew there were nothing we could say to make her understand the phenomenal changes we had experienced today. I looked down at my feet. Thank you my son for this precious gift of life, I thought.

After signing all the forms, the policemen took us back home. I looked around the rooms as if to find my son waiting for me. Tim whispered, "Baby, God gave us Sanato for eighteen years, now he has taken him back to be with him." He dried my tears away. I placed Sanato's shoes on the sofa. As we made arrangement our son's funeral, Tim replied, "we will bury our son besides his great grandparents." I nodded, "yes, that will be his final resting place." My body would not allow me to go any further. I stretched out besides Sanato's shoes. My lids were heavy and I fell asleep instantly. I dreamed Sanato was a little boy playing in a garden filled with laughter of other children. He stared at me with his big brown eyes. He shouted, "Mama, I'm home." I reached out for his hands. He replied, "no Mama, I don't want to leave. These are my friends." I cried out in my dream, "Sanato, Sanato, my baby, come to me." Tim woke me from my dream. "Maggie, Maggie wake up. You were calling Sanato's name." I explained my dream to Tim. He stated, "he's gone, Maggie, please pull yourself through this." I cried hysterically for hours.

The police report indicated that Sanato's accident was caused by heavy rain. He lost control of his car and crashed into the bridge. I knew what really happened. Sanato was 15 miles away from town. He had left home with the intention of finding Gail with her friends, but instead, he found her with another man. The hotel clerk gave a positive identification of my car being in the parking lot. She noticed my car when she came to work. My son drove around trying to forget the pain of finding Gail in the arms of another man. We won't ever know for sure what happened. But, sometimes a broken heart causes the soul to lose the ability to master our destiny.

We buried Sanato besides his great grandparents, and his dear friend, Bonnie. Six pallbearers carried the casket. Many mourners were sobbing quietly as they gathered at the funeral. No one questioned our glowing youthful appearance. They looked upon us as if the transformation had not occurred. As they placed my son's coffin on the bier, flowers were placed on top of the casket. What a beautiful day, I thought. The butterflies swarmed around the gravesite, high above the mourners. As they lowered the coffin into the ground, the wind drifted through the trees branches, making the sound of a musical tune. All of the mourners were attired in black except for the younger children. Gail and her family were there. She held her head down throughout the services. There were hundreds of tombstones in the graveyard, but Sanato's stone stood out like a beacon light.

After everyone left, Tim and I settled down with our hearts heavy with grief. We mourned the death of our son. Tim went to bed early, but I remained in the living room as if I was waiting for someone. Not knowing how to deal with the solitary feeling, I picked up Sanato's shoes. I couldn't depart with the thought that my son was dead. The lamplight flickered. I turned off the light thinking that maybe the bulb was going out. I walked towards the bedroom and glanced back at the shoes glowing in the dark. I was stunned by the glow and reached for the shoes grasping them to my chest. "Your spirit is here, my son. I feel your presence. The emptiness in my heart is reuniting my love with your spirit." Tim yelled, "Honey, are you okay?" I took a deep breath. I will keep this as our secret, my son, I thought. "Yes, I am okay," I answered as I entered the bedroom. Tim put his arms around me. My body and mind were tired. I drifted off to sleep.

The next morning Mrs. Green stayed close by my side providing comforting words of sympathy. She knew how heavy my heart was because she had lost her Bonnie only three years prior to this incident. Tim took time off from his

job to be with me. Mrs. Green began cleaning off the table.
She kept the house impeccable clean. She peeped around the
door. "Mrs. Carter, the sooner you remove Sanato's things
from the house, the better it will be for you." Gesturing
towards Sanato's shoes on the floor, she picked them up. I
jumped when she touched the shoes as if she had touched me
with a hot torch. Tim watched me with his eyes following my
every movement. Catching the stiffness in my voice, he
uttered, "Baby, are you okay. You look jittery. If you are not
ready to have Sanato's things removed from the house, we
can wait."

I waited a year before I allowed Mrs. Green to move
Sanato's belongings from the house. She begged me to go
shopping while she cleaned out his room. I had paced around
in Sanato's room looking over the glasses he had worn all of
his life. I convinced myself to let go of them. My son's tragic
death was a sorrowful time for us. The memories embedded
in our hearts would give animation to our lives. I knew that
when I returned from shopping, Mrs. Green would have
removed all of his belongings them from his room. My eyes
filled with tears as I picked up one of his trophies. Mrs.
Green interrupted, "Mrs. Carter, why don't you go ahead and
enjoy yourself. Let your mind relax for a little while. You
have not been out shopping for a long time." With a big hug
from her, I took her advice. I shopped for several hours. As I
returned, Mrs. Green greeted me at the door with a smile. I
wanted to rush right in to Sanato's room, but instead we
laughed at the bags I had in my hands. I gave Mrs. Green
several large shopping bags filled with clothes. She beamed,

"gee...ugh...is all of this for me?" "Everything in those bags belongs to you. Take them home and try them on, I requested." She stared with an uncertain excitement on her face. She stammered, "now Mrs. Carter, ugh...I hope you understand. I...ugh...took all of Sanato's clothes and things to the Salvation Army." She was waiting for me to breakdown in tears. She continued, "I am sure someone will find lots of use for his clothes and things." A sad ton knotted in my voice as I managed to respond, "I am happy you removed his things." Mrs. Green frowned, searching my face for a more truthful reply. "Did you give Sanato's shoes away? Looking on the floor for them, Mrs. Green suggested, "I thought you had put them away. I didn't see them after you left." I began looking for the shoes myself. We couldn't find the shoes anywhere in the house.

Mrs. Green said goodnight. As she walked out the door, she glanced back and said, "maybe you put up the shoes and forgot where you placed them. "No, I thought to myself. I didn't put the shoes away." I searched the house over and over again, but yet, no shoes. Wherever Sanato's shoes are, his spirit will prevail. We sold Sanato's car to one of his friends that was moving far away. Gail and her family moved away also, and we never saw her again after the funeral.

Tim and I became very active in our benevolence program, helping people less fortunate than we were. Tim became a full time supporter for the homeless group. We stayed busy even though we were getting up in age. The gift from our son gave us a new lease on life. We both looked ten years younger. We didn't understand how it came to be, nor do other people. There is no answer to how Sanato was able to restore our youth. We live each day as if it is our last day and tomorrow does not exist. The recollections of our son will remain in our hearts forever. Being deprived of our son has caused emptiness in our life...which will linger in our souls. The power of love will forever shine around us, enlightening the pathway made by the footsteps of Sanato Kareen Carter.

The End